Rescued by the ALIEN Hit Man

VILLAINS DO IT BETTER

TERRYN MARS

Rescued By The Alien Hit Man
Villains Do It Better

by Terryn Mars
All rights reserved

ePub ISBN: 978-1-7770055-8-0

Print ISBN: 978-1-7770055-9-7

CHAPTER 1
MIA

The air in the Dufair jungle thrummed with life, charged with the energy of the countless bioluminescent plants that made Talamhmar's moon a hot spot for scientists and botanists. I knelt beside a cluster of iridescent ferns that shimmered like a field of stars in the dark jungle, their fronds flowing with a soft green light. My fingers danced over their glowing fronds. Each touch sent a shiver up my spine—these were unlike anything we'd seen before. With precise movements, I extracted a fragile, luminescent specimen.

The ground was soft and damp beneath me, the recent rain accentuating the lush aroma of moss and the heady scent of alien blossoms. The jungle canopy above bathed me in ethereal light, casting the world around in hues of haunting blues and purples. Each plant cradled secrets within its radiant leaves—secrets I was determined to unlock.

Excitement skittered through me at finally being on Dufair. After months of begging my boss to let us get in some field work, he'd finally allowed Amund and me to venture to the moon for research.

"Remarkable, isn't it?" Amund's voice pulled me from my silent reverie. "These ferns could revolutionize our understanding of bioluminescence."

"Absolutely," I said without looking up, my hands steady as I placed the sample into a container. "This one has an enzyme I've never seen before. It might revolutionize bioluminescent energy."

"Ah, Mia, always thinking of the next big discovery." His laughter was a warm blanket in the coolness of the moon's evening. "I'll scout ahead for more."

"Be careful," I said, watching his retreating figure dissolve into the vibrant thicket.

If my parents had still been alive, they'd have made the next big discovery. Once part of a family of three scientists hoping to find cures for disease and uncover alternative forms of energy, now it was just me.

Time slipped away as I continued my meticulous collecting, each new specimen more fascinating than the last. The jungle's symphony was a constant backdrop—the rustle of leaves, distant calls of unseen creatures, the hum of life itself. But suddenly, an unsettling silence fell. The usual chorus of the jungle ceased, as if holding its breath. My ears strained for the familiar rustle of leaves or the distant calls of the jungle's inhabitants, but there was nothing. Only a void where sound should have been.

"Amund?" My voice sliced through the stillness. No response, just the echo of my anxiety. I stood up, my heart hammering against my ribs. I tried again, louder. "Amund!"

Still nothing. Panic clawed at my chest, as I realized even the guards' chatter had vanished. "Guards!" I called out, hoping one of the guards my employer insisted I bring with me would answer. Silence mocked me.

As I turned in a slow circle, every shadow seemed to pulse with unseen threats. My breaths came quick, my skin prickling with the anticipation of danger. A suffocating panic threatened to take hold, but I forced myself to take calming breaths. What if Amund was hurt and needed me?

"Guards!" Still nothing.

The quiet held a menace now, a prelude to a nightmare I couldn't wake from. My hand closed over the hilt of the small utility knife I carried—pitiful against what might lurk beyond the glow.

"Amund, this isn't funny," I said to the dark, knowing full well he wouldn't play such tricks.

I took a step forward, my mind racing. Should I seek shelter? Or find Amund and the others? But before I could decide, shadows shifted, and the night erupted into chaos.

The luminescent flora dimmed as if to hide from the terror that tore through the tranquil scene. A battle cry shattered the stillness, and slavers burst forth from the underbrush, their figures grotesque parodies in the bioluminescent glow.

The leader's silhouette was unmistakable—the scars on his face catching what little light there was, making him a specter of violence incarnate. His men swarmed the clearing with the confidence of predators who had cornered their prey.

"Amund!" I screamed, hoping against hope he'd answer, that he'd somehow escaped notice. But my heart sank as I heard his voice cut short by a choked-off cry of pain.

I stumbled back, tripping over a root, my knife scattered to the ground. My palms hit the soft dirt, the damp soil cold and unforgiving. The slavers were upon us, their guttural language filling the air as they rounded up their quarry.

Then I saw him—Amund—falling to the ground a hundred meters away from me. A gash along his neck had turned his field shirt a dark rust. His eyes met mine in one final, desperate plea before the life drained from them. Something inside me tore away with his departing gaze.

"Amund!" I screamed, but my voice was lost in the chaos. Blood spattered across the glowing plants, their light dimming under the grim reality of violence. The slavers turned their attention to me next, their eyes gleaming with malice.

"Please, no," I said, backing away until I felt the rough bark of a tree press against my spine. My mind filled with visions of capture, of enslavement, and worse. I'd rather die here, on this foreign moon, than endure whatever horrors awaited at the hands of these monsters.

"Get her!" The leader barked, his voice cutting through the air like a knife. The slavers lunged at me, and I braced myself for the end.

But as I cowered, waiting for the end, out of the shadows a shape detached itself from the darkness—a towering figure with skin the colour of bittersweet nightshade. Eyes that glowed with a fierce, unnatural yellow locked onto mine, mesmerizing and terrifying all at once. His presence alone commanded my terror-stricken attention.

He moved like a wraith, a silent storm of vengeance. Each motion was purposeful, each strike precise. Slavers fell before him, their cries ending abruptly. He was like death incarnate, and yet, in that moment, he was the most beautiful thing I'd ever seen.

"Stay down," he ordered, his voice low and resonant. It vibrated through the chaos, anchoring me to life even as everything else spelled certain death.

"Who—" was all I managed before he was upon them again, a whirlwind of deadly intent.

A slaver lunged for me, eyes alight with malice, but the mysterious savior intercepted, dispatching my would-be captor with a swift, almost casual efficiency. His movements were a blur, a symphony of violence performed with the precision of a master.

"Who are you?" I asked, clutching at the dirt, trying to find my bearings amid the bedlam.

"Cikarius Vex," he said, without looking at me, his attention fixed on the remaining threats.

Then, as he surveyed the area for any lingering dangers, he stooped beside one of the fallen slavers. The moon's bioluminescent glow painted his violet skin in surreal shades. His hand emerged, clutching an object that he promptly shoved into a side pocket of his leather pants.

"Come," Cikarius said once the immediate danger had passed. "We have to get out of here now."

"Amund." I said, glancing at the still form of my colleague. A part of me wanted to run to him, to see if there was any hope, but deep down, I knew the truth.

Cikarius shook his head. "He's gone." His gaze scanned the area for more threats. "We have to move. Now."

"I need to gather all that I can." I pointed at the laptop, the samples, the equipment that belonged to my employer. Employee safety was their top priority, that's why Amund and I had guards with us, but the samples plus my research would be worth a million credits.

He gave a curt nod, surveying the area for threats. I rushed around, gathering everything I could fit in the backpack, hoping it wouldn't slow me down too much. Cikarius was decidedly more fit than I was. A trek through the jungle wouldn't even raise his heartbeat, I guessed.

"Ready?" he asked.

I nodded, tears pooling in my eyes when I glanced over at Amund's prone form on the jungle floor.

Cikarius's hand extended toward me, an unspoken promise of protection. I hesitated only for a second—survival was a powerful motivator. With Amund gone and our guards likely dead, Cikarius was my lifeline in this neon nightmare.

I placed my trembling hand in his, feeling the strength in

his grip. As we ran, I dared to glance back at the carnage. And though I knew I should feel nothing but fear, something else fluttered within me—an inexplicable sense of connection to this enigmatic stranger who had become my guardian in the dark.

We weaved through luminescent underbrush, the eerie glow of Dufair's flora casting our shadows in a haunting dance against the dense foliage. Cikarius moved with an animal grace that belied his imposing frame, every muscle and sinew orchestrated to perfection. My breath came in ragged gasps, partly from exertion, partly from something far more primal as I watched the play of muscles under Cikarius's form fitting clothing.

"Thank you," I said, my voice barely above a whisper as we paused beneath the shelter of an overhanging fern, its fronds shimmering like a chandelier of soft green light.

"Don't thank me yet," he said, his gaze scanning the jungle perimeter, those yellow eyes piercing through the darkness and, it seemed, right into my very soul.

He pulled out the small tablet he'd taken from the slaver and his body tensed—a reaction so subtle, yet so at odds with his previous composure that my heart skipped a beat. What could unsettle such a man? He turned the object over in his hands, his expression unreadable. I swallowed the fear rising in my throat and stepped closer, driven by a mix of dread and curiosity.

"Is something wrong?" My voice was steady, but inside, I was anything but.

He didn't reply immediately, his focus fixed on whatever he'd found. The silence stretched between us, punctuated only by the distant cry of some nocturnal predator.

I studied him. A muscle in his jaw clenched. His hands clutched the tablet. A war waged in his eyes, and I wondered if he would reveal what troubled him. His gaze finally met mine, the weight of concern in his eyes evident. Whatever revelation awaited me, our troubles were far from over.

He extended his hand, revealing the tablet, an image illuminated on its cracked screen. It was me—my photo, unmistakably captured in the sterile light of the Deiridh Airm Solutions research lab on Alfataken Station. My breath hitched, and an icy shiver ran down my spine.

Alfataken Station had security issues. What massive space station didn't? But security at Deiridh Airm Solutions was beyond tight. Especially the research lab. How had someone infiltrated the lab and taken my picture?

"What does this mean?" I asked, though my voice quivered like a leaf in a storm.

Cikarius's nod directed my gaze to the path we'd taken away from the lifeless form of Amund, my colleague and friend, now just a memory against the vibrant backdrop of Dufair's flora. "This was no random attack on scientists. You were the target."

Shock rippled through me, followed by a wave of nausea, freezing me in place. A target? But why? I had always been amicable, never one to stir up trouble or incite animosity among my peers.

"Everyone likes me," I said, the words sounding feeble even to my own ears.

"Obviously someone doesn't. Hiring slavers isn't cheap or easy. Whoever did this has resources and a vendetta," he said. "Did you piss anyone off lately?"

"No," I replied, a sense of helplessness creeping in. "I can't think of anyone who would—"

He looked me over slowly, his yellow eyes locking onto mine with an intensity that made my stomach flip. He examined me from head to toe, and warmth bloomed beneath my skin where his gaze lingered. It was a look that stripped away the layers, seeing beyond the scientist, the botanist…seeing me. Heat spread through me, igniting every nerve ending. Something about the way he looked at me—predatory, assessing—made my pulse quicken.

"Turn anyone down lately?" he asked, his voice low, almost intimate.

My heart pounded as memories of polite rejections given to well-meaning colleagues flashed through my mind. "No, the scientists on my team are gentlemen." But Cikarius was far from a gentleman, and a part of me—a reckless, untamed part—found that thrilling.

"Obviously, not everyone in your life is as agreeable," he said, folding the tablet and slipping it into his pocket.

His presence enveloped me, a mix of danger and enigma. The air buzzed with tension, charged by the ferocity of his protection and the aura of mystery that clung to him like a second skin.

"Then what do we do?" My voice wavered between fear and something else—something darker, more primal.

"First, we get out of here alive," he said, extending his hand towards me and I took it. His touch was electric, sending a shiver of arousal up my spine. Was it wrong to feel safe in the presence of someone so deadly?

I realized then, standing in the afterglow of violence and the shadow of death, how drawn I was to this man—a stranger who'd saved me, yet held the power to unravel my very existence. And as fear and desire tangled within me, I recognized that my world had shifted, irrevocably altered by the gravity of his yellow eyes.

"Time's not on our side." Cikarius's voice cut through the stillness, a stark reminder of the danger shadowing us. "You need to come with me if you want to survive."

"Where are we going?" I asked, my voice barely more than a whisper, trying to keep up with his long strides.

"To safety," he said, his grip firm. His skin was cool against mine, a stark contrast to the heat coursing through my body. Every brush of our hands sent sparks of electricity through me, heightening my awareness of him, of us.

I yanked my hand out of his grasp and instantly missed

the connection. My instinct was to protest, to demand answers, but his next words froze them on my tongue. "Your guards are dead. Amund is dead. There are more slavers out there."

The weight of reality settled on my shoulders, heavy and cold. My hands trembled, not from the evening's chill, but from the palpable threat that lingered like poison in the air.

"Why me?" I asked, not expecting an answer. The warmth of his hand was reassuring, grounding me amidst the chaos.

"Speculations can wait," he said, his tone brooking no argument. "Right now, focus on surviving."

Survival. It sounded so simple, yet it weighed heavily on me. With every step deeper into the jungle, I felt the enormity of what had happened—and what could still happen. My mind raced with questions that had no immediate answers, my body reacting instinctively to the man beside me who had saved my life with such deadly precision.

Cikarius extended his hand. An invitation—a lifeline—in the growing darkness. I hesitated, staring at his open palm. Could I trust this man? His capacity for violence was undeniable, his efficiency terrifying. Yet, those same hands had dispatched my would-be captors without a second thought.

A shiver that wasn't entirely fear traced down my spine as I placed my hand in his. The contact sparked a shock of arousal, an inexplicable yearning for the strength that now encased my own. I wondered if safety was an illusion, a fleeting comfort in the arms of a killer.

His grip tightened, pulling me closer as we navigated through the dense underbrush. The proximity brought a flood of sensations—his cool skin against mine, the rhythmic rise and fall of his chest, the intoxicating mix of danger and safety that he exuded. I leaned into his presence, drawn to the enigma that he represented.

"Stay close," he said, his breath hot against my ear.

"Of course," I whispered back, feeling a heady mix of fear

and arousal. If anyone could keep me safe, it was him, but the question gnawed at me—would I be safe from him?

As we continued tromping through the jungle, I made a silent vow: If I survived this ordeal, I'd confine myself to the sterile halls of Alfataken Station. No more fieldwork, no more risks.

CHAPTER 2
CIKARIUS

The jungle of Dufair cloaked me in shadows as I followed a faint trail, my senses sharp beneath the luminescent canopy. The air was thick with the heady scent of alien flora, damp dirt clawing at my nostrils. Bioluminescent leaves above me cast a ghostly glow on the ground below, illuminating the lifeless bodies of several guards. A female voice pierced the silence, fear palpable as she yelled, "Amund!"

Something stirred within me, an unfamiliar sensation that defied my calculated nature. I paused for a moment, allowing the silence of the jungle to swallow any sound I might have made.

"Guards!" Her voice came again, more desperate this time. Glancing over my shoulder at the lifeless bodies of men strewn across the mossy ground, I knew these guards wouldn't be able to help her. And neither could I, not really. She called for protectors who could no longer answer, and I was a phantom on a mission, bound by an objective that allowed no detours.

Yet, as the woman's cry echoed, a protective instinct I

never experienced before coiled tight in my chest. There was no logic in it—the Violet Phantom did not stray from his path. But the emotion was there, as real as the grip of my blade and the thrill of the hunt that usually surged through my veins.

Her scent wafted towards me, blending with the fragrant aroma of the jungle. It wasn't the sickly-sweet scent of most beings; hers had a unique quality, like courage hidden beneath layers of fear. My genetically engineered instincts urged me to continue, despite the conflicting emotions swirling within me. The mission came first.

With each step closer to her, desire clawed its way to the surface, threatening to consume me. I burst through the tangled curtain of vines and towering ferns, my senses acutely tuned to the unfolding chaos ahead. The sight of her cowering form only intensified the feeling. Mia Clarke - a woman whose very existence challenged everything I thought I knew. Rich brown hair pulled into a ponytail swished as she scrabbled away from the slavers. Her green eyes, like a sea I longed to drown in, beckoned me closer. A metal pendant nestled in the hollow of her neck caught the bioluminescent light. Her fear should have been intoxicating, should have sharpened the thrill of the hunt. Instead, it summoned a fierce need to protect that I hadn't known existed within me. My long line of assassin ancestors bred out chivalrous feelings long ago.

"Stay down," I said, my voice low and authoritative, barely audible over the cacophony of alien calls and the slavers' grunts.

In a dance of deadly grace, I moved among the slavers. My hands, precise instruments of destruction, disarmed one, snapped the neck of another. Each movement was practiced, honed by countless missions, as I became an avatar of death in the luminescent wilds.

The fear in the slavers' eyes fed me, a dark satisfaction

that they recognized the predator before them. They were no match for me, and deep down, they knew it. The realization flickered across their faces just before I sent them into the endless void.

Despite the efficiency of my work, a part of me, a part that had awakened upon hearing Mia's distress, wondered why these learned scientists kept coming to Dufair. Didn't they know the dangers lurking beneath the beauty of these glowing canopies?

As the last of the slavers fell before me, his body crumpling to the mossy floor, I turned back to Mia. She lay there, trembling, her ponytail askew, those enchanting green eyes locked onto mine. Fear emanated from her, but instead of fueling the hunter within, her vulnerability sparked something to life inside me.

"Who are you?" Mia asked, her voice trembling with fear and curiosity.

"Cikarius Vex," I said, my tone steady despite the storm brewing within me.

Kneeling, I rifled through the leader of the slavers' pockets, seeking anything of value or information. My fingers found the cool surface of a tablet, and I activated the screen with a touch. A familiar face stared back at me—Mia Clarke— her name emblazoned beneath her photo. I swore under my breath. This changed everything.

I shoved the tablet into a side pocket of my leather pants. "Come. We have to get out of here now."

She whispered the name she had yelled before. Her murdered colleague.

"He's gone. We have to move. Now."

Something passed over her face. Acceptance maybe. I'd seen it a thousand times in victims who knew there was no way to escape their fate. She insisted on taking things with us. Things that would weigh us down, but I couldn't deny her. I gave her a nod, and she leapt up, gathered everything she could, and shoved it into a large backpack.

"Ready? I asked.

She nodded, and I offered my hand, hoping she would take it, but also wishing she wouldn't. A touch might spark something more primal in me, something I had no idea how to fight. These urges weren't supposed to exist in me.

Her small hand was cool against mine. As we moved through the jungle, I wondered how long it would take to convince Mia that she would be safer with me. Time wasn't on our side, and the slavers would send more. The urge to claim her, to make her mine, threatened to overwhelm me at every turn.

"Thank you," she said.

I turned to look at her. It was a mistake. Cheeks flushed pink from exertion, her hair askew with tendrils that had escaped the ponytail framing her face, and bright green eyes shining at me like I wasn't a killing machine, but a savior twisted my heart. The need to feel her writhing beneath me overpowered the programming of my hunter instinct. Two survival instincts warring with each other. The need to survive and the need to procreate.

"Don't thank me yet," I said.

To push thoughts of Mia moaning beneath me from my mind, I pulled out the tablet I'd stolen from the slavers and swore again.

"Is something wrong?"

Everything. Life as I knew it flashed before me. Failing this mission meant exile from the Sionagog Syndicate and likely a hit squad. The most notorious assassins' guild in the sector, the Sionagog Syndicate, didn't take failure lightly. They'd paid handsomely for genetically engineered killers. Killers that never missed, never failed, never rescued their quarry.

I handed the tablet to her.

She gasped. "What does this mean?"

I nodded toward the path we'd taken. "This was no random attack on scientists. You were the target."

Her eyes widened. "Everyone likes me."

I could see why everyone should like her. Despite the danger, determination shone in her eyes. Dirt marred her face, but couldn't hide her beauty. Poetic thoughts like that would get us both killed if I wasn't careful.

"Obviously someone doesn't. Hiring slavers isn't cheap or easy. Whoever did this has resources and a vendetta. Did you piss anyone off lately?"

"No," she said. "I can't think of anyone who would—"

I raked my gaze over her. Taking in every curve of her body, my gaze settled first on her plump breasts, heaving under her shirt from the exertion of traversing the jungle. Thanks to my enhanced vision and special awareness, plus the creativity added to all engineered killers, I could picture her without her clothes and my mouth went dry.

"Turn anyone down lately?" I asked, cursing the desire evident in my voice. Maybe she wouldn't notice.

"No, the scientists on my team are gentlemen."

Gentlemen. The word echoed in my mind, a stark contrast to the bloodshed that had brought us here. I wondered how she'd react to someone like me, someone crafted from violence and shadows. As I pondered this, I noted the subtle changes in her—her breathing slightly quicker, pupils dilated —not just from shock, but from something more. The protective instinct that had awakened within me roared to life once more, urging me to shield her from the dangers that lurked all around us.

"Obviously, not everyone in your life is as agreeable," I said, sliding the tablet back into my pocket.

"Then what do we do?" she asked.

"First, we get out of here alive," I said.

I offered Mia my hand, half hoping she would reject it. But she put her small trembling hand in mine, sending a bolt of arousal through my body. My mission had been to eliminate her, but now I would do anything to protect her. And so, for the first time since becoming a hit man, I would fail.

CHAPTER 3
MIA

I followed Cikarius through the dense jungle, my heart pounding in my chest as we navigated the treacherous terrain. He moved with the grace and agility of a predator, blending seamlessly into the alien environment. Every so often, he would stop and motion for me to hide behind a tree or some other form of cover. I couldn't help but feel a sense of gratitude towards him for saving me from those slavers, but I couldn't shake the feeling that there was more to him than met the eye. Why was he just strolling through the jungle on Dufair? It was mostly scientists and their guards here, after all. Could I really trust him completely?

As we continued our journey, the eerie sounds of the jungle filled my ears–strange calls from unseen creatures echoing through the dense foliage, and the soft rustle of leaves suggesting hidden movement all around us. The air was thick with the scent of exotic flowers mingling with damp soil, while towering trees with bioluminescent leaves cast a surreal glow on everything they touched.

My mind raced with questions about why someone would hire slavers to capture me. Were they going to kill me, or simply abduct me? Thankfully, I never got to find out because Cikarius had intervened. At the thought of his muscular arms enveloping me, my body shivered with a sudden wetness in my core, and I wondered how rough he might be, if given the chance.

"Keep moving," he said. His voice was low and commanding. I nodded, forcing myself to focus on staying alive and following his lead.

The sensation of danger was palpable, like a living, breathing entity surrounding us. Still, as we ventured deeper into the jungle, I couldn't help but admire its beauty. The vibrant colors and unique flora were breathtaking, unlike anything I'd ever seen before. And somehow, Cikarius blended in seamlessly, as if he were a part of this alien world.

"Watch your step," he warned, his glowing yellow eyes scanning our surroundings for any potential threats. I swallowed hard, my pulse quickening at the thought of what else might be lurking in the shadows.

We pressed on, determined to find shelter before nightfall. With each passing moment, my attraction to Cikarius intensified, despite my lingering reservations. I needed him to survive, but I couldn't ignore the fire that burned within me, threatening to consume us both. Sensual thoughts of him ricocheted in my mind, and I needed to get my mind off how it would feel to have his hands roaming my body.

"Can I see the tablet again with the photo of me?" I asked, my voice barely audible above the cacophony of alien jungle sounds.

"Why?" he asked, his tone sharp and direct. "Someone wanted you dead or captured. Why do you need to see the photo again?"

"I just… I just do," I said, hesitant but adamant.

With a sigh, Cikarius pulled out the tablet and handed it to me. As our fingers touched, a sizzle went through me like an electric shock, leaving me breathless and craving more of his touch. So much for getting those thoughts out of my mind.

I examined the image, a snapshot of my life before this chaos began. It was taken right after I had made a breakthrough in my research project. The discovery had been so significant that Amund and I had come to Dufair to gather more specimens for testing. The timing couldn't be a coincidence. Someone, somewhere, wanted me silenced.

"Could this have something to do with someone hiring slavers to capture me?" I asked, the thought chilling me to the bone.

Cikarius gave me a doubtful look, but there was something in his eyes–a flicker of calculation, as if he were piecing together some hidden puzzle. "What are you thinking?" I asked.

"Nothing," he said, too quickly. "We need to keep moving."

It wasn't nothing, but I nodded. If we got through this, I would press him for more details later.

As we continued deeper into the jungle, the sense of danger around us grew stronger, the shadows darker and more menacing. But Cikarius never faltered, leading us through the treacherous terrain with the skill and precision of a predator.

As we continued our journey, I couldn't help but marvel at how easily Cikarius navigated the dense foliage. He moved with a grace and precision that belied his formidable strength, as if he were an extension of the jungle itself. And though I had seen others of his kind on Alfataken Station, everyone gave them a wide berth–a fact that only added to the mystery and danger surrounding him. Rumors floated in the air, through the ducts on the station, that those like Cikarius were hired killers.

As we moved deeper into the jungle, my foot caught on a tangled mass of foliage. I stumbled forward, but before I could hit the ground, Cikarius's powerful arms were around me, holding me securely against his firm body. Warmth seeped into every part of me that was in contact with him, and my knees went weak.

Heat pooled between my legs as his nose flared, and he stared down at me intently. His mouth was so close to mine that I could feel his breath on my lips. "Be careful," he warned, righting me before taking a step back. "We need to hurry."

"Where are we going?" I asked, my voice trembling slightly from the proximity of our bodies.

"We need to find shelter," he said, his eyes scanning our surroundings. "See if we can stay off the slavers' radar." He raked his gaze over me, making me shiver. "I don't suppose you have anything in that equipment you made us bring along that is more appropriate to wear?"

Though I had a jacket in the backpack, I shook my head. If my appearance unnerved him even a little, I'd take that advantage. "No," I lied, hoping he wouldn't press further.

He nodded curtly and turned, continuing to lead the way through the dense undergrowth. We pressed on, the ever-present sounds of the jungle keeping us on edge. I was grateful for Cikarius's presence, but I couldn't shake the feeling that I should be wary, yet I found myself irresistibly drawn to him, longing to know more about the man beneath the stoic façade.

As we trekked onward, the vulnerability I felt, both physically and emotionally, in this alien world pressed in on me. My life had been turned upside down, and now I depended on a mysterious stranger for my survival. But despite the uncertainty and danger that surrounded us, one thing became crystal clear: my attraction to Cikarius had become impossible to ignore.

And as the shadows lengthened and the jungle's biolumi-nescent canopy cast an eerie glow around us, I swore that if we survived this ordeal, I would do everything in my power to explore the connection between us–to feel alive in his arms, writhing beneath him like never before.

As we ventured deeper into the jungle, my senses became more attuned to our surroundings. The damp soil squelching beneath my feet, the humidity clinging to my skin, and the unique fragrance of alien flowers filling my nostrils. The vibrant colors from the bioluminescent canopy above us cast a surreal glow on the foliage, making it difficult to discern genuine threats from mere shadows.

My unease grew as I sensed movement nearby. The hairs on the back of my neck stood up, alerting me to the danger that lurked just out of sight My heart raced, and I struggled to breathe, the weight of fear settling on my chest.

"Stop," he said, grabbing my arm to halt my progress. He looked at me, his eyes narrowing in concern as he scanned the environment.

Suddenly, I came face to face with a laghairt. Its menacing presence sent a jolt of fear through me, paralyzing me where I stood. The creature, a blend of reptilian scales and mammalian fur covering its muscular body, stood on powerful hind legs with a long tail for balance. Its sharp, alert eyes locked onto mine, and razor-sharp teeth filled its mouth.

Unable to move or react, my mind raced with panic and desperation. One wrong move could prove fatal. But just as the creature lunged toward me, Cikarius sprang into action, swiftly intervening to protect me.

His movements were fluid and deadly, a lethal dance born from years of training and honed instincts. He expertly dodged and countered the creature's strikes, using his formidable strength and agility to keep me safe. I watched in awe as Cikarius showcased his protective nature, fighting with every ounce of his being to ensure our survival.

As he finally gained the upper hand, overpowering the laghairt and driving it away from us, I couldn't help but feel a surge of gratitude mixed with relief. My heart pounded in my chest, and my breath came in ragged gasps as I tried to process what had just happened. Cikarius turned to face me, his eyes filled with concern.

"Are you alright?" he asked, his voice softening ever so slightly.

I nodded, swallowing hard as I tried to regain my composure. "Yes, thanks to you," I said. "You saved my life. Again."

He simply nodded, his glowing yellow eyes locked onto mine, as if searching for something deeper within me. The intensity of his gaze made my knees go weak, and I had to fight the urge to reach out and touch him–to feel the heat of his skin against mine and know that he was as real as the danger we had just faced.

As we continued on, my mind raced with conflicting emotions. I was growing increasingly dependent on Cikarius for protection, and part of me worried about what that meant for my survival. Was it wise to rely so heavily on someone who was still a stranger to me?

And yet, my attraction to him intensified with each passing moment. His strength, his skill, his unwavering determination to keep me safe... all of it fueled the fire that burned within me. My body ached with desire for him, and I longed for the moment when we could finally give in to the passion that threatened to consume me.

But there were more pressing matters at hand. We needed to find shelter and stay off the slavers' radar–or whatever alien technology they used to track their prey. And though the thought of being alone with Cikarius in some hidden refuge stirred a delicious thrill within me, we couldn't afford to let our guard down or succumb to our baser instincts. Not yet, anyway.

"Where are we going?" I asked, trying to focus on the task

at hand and ignore the heat that spread through my body at the mere thought of him.

"Somewhere safe," he said, his voice low and measured. "We need to stay hidden until we can figure out who wants you dead or captured… and why."

CHAPTER 4
CIKARIUS

As we cautiously approached the hidden cave, the soft moss-covered ground muffled our footsteps. I was grateful to have found this sanctuary. The jungle moon held a lot of secrets. Numerous ways to die, but also several sanctuaries like the cave. You just needed to know where to look. "Stay put," I said, not wanting to leave Mia's side, but it was unavoidable.

Her eyes widened, pleading. "You're leaving me?"

The instinct to comfort her almost overwhelmed me. "Only for a minute. I need to make sure nothing can find us."

She nodded and I left the cave before I changed my mind. With my heightened senses and knowledge of the environment, I set up an early notification system using vines and fallen branches to alert us if anyone or anything approached our hiding place.

Slipping back into the cave, my eyes scanned the surroundings, ensuring our safety before allowing myself to settle down. Every bio enhancement and engineered gene in my body screamed that this was the moment I should kill Mia. Her body would never be found. I had barely discovered the cave myself, so I knew no one else would be able to find it. But I had saved her life twice now, and all I wanted was to feel her curves and plunge deep inside her.

"Is it safe?" Mia asked, her green eyes filled with a mix of curiosity and concern, her voice soft-spoken yet precise.

"Safe enough for now," I said, my tone measured. I couldn't help but admire her keen intelligence as she observed our hideout, her slender form clothed in attire suitable for fieldwork in the stifling jungle of Dufair, but clung to her body in such a way that I wanted to rip it off.

I forced myself to remain still, fighting the urge to act on my genetic programming. Mia's life was in my hands now, twice over. The thought should have filled me with satisfaction at a job well done. Instead, it left a bitter taste in my mouth.

Mia approached me with slow, cautious steps, her slender form melting into the gloom. I watched the gentle rise and fall of her chest, the soft curve of her hips as they swayed with each stride. Heat pooled in my abdomen at the sight, my body responding to her nearness in a way no one had programmed it to.

"Thank you," she said, her voice barely above a whisper. "For saving me again."

The soft scent of her arousal reached me, and I fought the urge to act on it. I grunted in response, unsure of how to process the conflicting impulses warring within me. My fingers curled into fists, nails biting into genetically engineered, quick healing flesh as I fought to remain still.

Genetically engineered for efficiency and obedience, an awakening conscience led me to question my existence and purpose. As I sat there, watching Mia explore our temporary refuge, I realized that my protective instincts toward her had solidified my commitment to her. But what kind of future could we have together? The weight of my doubts and fears threatened to crush me.

"Are you okay?" she asked, her green eyes searching mine with a newfound vulnerability. "You seem… distant."

I hesitated before responding, knowing that I couldn't reveal the truth of my turmoil. "I'm fine," I lied, forcing a smile. "Just tired from our journey."

"Me too," she said, and for a moment, we shared an understanding that went beyond words. The air between us crackled with tension as we acknowledged our mutual attraction—despite the danger that surrounded us.

But my desire for her would have to remain unfulfilled. As much as I longed to touch her, to feel her body pressed against mine, I couldn't allow myself that pleasure. I was a hit man, after all—a being created for destruction, not love.

"Are you sure you're okay?" Mia asked again, her concern for me evident in her voice. I could hear the pounding of her heart and smell her arousal, but I couldn't let my own desires distract me from our precarious situation.

"Trust me, Mia," I said, trying to reassure her while avoiding the full truth. "I'm fine. We just need to stay focused on staying safe."

She nodded, but there was a hint of disappointment in her eyes. It was clear she sensed something more beneath the surface, but she didn't push further. Instead, she moved closer, her slender fingers brushing against my hand. The contact sent a jolt of electric arousal through me, and I struggled to maintain control.

"I don't know why you're helping me," she said, "but I'm grateful you did."

"Your gratitude is unnecessary," I said, my voice strained with suppressed emotion. "It's my duty to protect you."

"Is that all it is?" she asked, her gaze locked on mine. "Just a duty?"

My throat tightened as I considered how to respond. Could I admit the depth of my desire for her? That every fiber of my being screamed for me to claim her as my own?

"Maybe not," I said, my voice barely audible. "But that doesn't change the fact that I'm dangerous, Mia. You should be careful around me."

"Even an honorable man would have made love to me by now," she said, her emerald eyes darkening with desire. Her words, like a siren's call, tempted me to lose myself in her embrace. But I couldn't give in—not when so much was at stake.

"Please, Mia," I said, my voice hoarse with longing. "Don't make this harder than it already is."

Her hand found mine in the dark, slender fingers threading between my own. A jolt passed through me at her touch, lightning dancing across nerve endings no ordinary human possessed. I stared at our joined hands, uncertainty gnawing at the edges of my thoughts.

This was dangerous. She was dangerous. I should end this now before—

Warm lips pressed against my chest, chasing the trail of scars that marked my skin. Scars that not even my quick healing flesh could eradicate. One scar for each completed mission. A groan rumbled in my throat as sparks ignited under her mouth, racing through my body to pool in my groin.

"Be with me," she said against my skin. "Just for tonight."

"I will be in this cave with you all night."

A smile turned up the corners of her mouth. "You know that's not what I meant."

The air in the cave crackled with tension as Mia rubbed my hardening cock through my pants. Her touch broke me. I growled, overcome by the intensity of my desire, and moved with lightning speed, gently placing Mia on the soft soil in the cave while I straddled her. She smiled, writhing beneath me, her body begging for my touch.

"I hope you're not that fast with everything you do."

As I quickly disrobed, Mia's eyes widened with curiosity

when she saw my chest. Anyone who had ever seen it wondered at the marks, but her gaze traveled lower and stopped at my cock. Her tongue darted out to touch her lips, and I could feel the heat from her lustful stare.

"Not everything," I said.

I wanted to rip Mia's clothes off, but this would be my only chance to be with her. I wanted to savor the moment. Slowly, I undressed her, each article of clothing sliding off her body like sensual torture for both of us. I kissed her flesh as I revealed it, feeling her shiver beneath my touch.

Once Mia lay naked beneath me, vulnerable and beautiful, I still waited. I wanted to worship her body, to explore every inch of her before I claimed her as my own. My fingers traced delicate patterns on her skin, igniting a fire that spread throughout our entwined bodies.

I claimed her lips in a searing kiss that left my cock twitching with need. My tongue swept into her mouth, dueling with hers, the velvety strokes sending sparks of need through me. Her hands roamed my body as if she couldn't get enough of me, setting my skin ablaze wherever she touched. I groaned into her mouth, desire burning in my veins like molten fire.

My eyes flicked open for a moment and in the dim light of the cave, I saw the impossible.

My skin seemed to glow as if lit from within, pulsing with a subtle bioluminescence in time with the pounding of her heart. Each place her hands trailed on my body left behind fleeting bursts of color, as if her very touch could ignite my augmented cells. A fated mate. It wasn't supposed to be possible.

Mesmerized, I broke the kiss to trail kisses down Mia's body, stopping at her breasts to suck both like a man dying of thirst. I loved the way she moaned, a symphony of pleasure that reverberated through my very soul. Moving lower, I pressed tender kisses on her belly, feeling her muscles quiver beneath my touch.

The scent of her arousal filled my senses, an intoxicating perfume I couldn't get enough of. I slid lower until I reached the dark curls at the apex of her thighs.

"Please, Cikarius," she said, a note of pleading in her voice.

Settling between her legs, my breath hitched as I beheld the sight before me. The scent of her arousal was intoxicating and irresistible. Gently, I licked her clit, coaxing a gasp from her lips.

She cried out, back bowing off the ground as I dove in with abandon. My tongue swirled and flicked over her clit, delving into her entrance to gather more of her sweet nectar. I could feast on her for hours, addicted to the sounds of her pleasure and the way she writhed beneath my ministrations.

Her hands fisted in my hair, holding me in place as her hips undulated. I increased the pressure, wrapping my lips around her sensitive bud to suck strongly. She screamed my name, inner walls clenching around nothing as her orgasm crashed over her in waves.

I gentled my touch but didn't stop, lapping at her entrance through each aftershock. When her grip on my hair loosened, I kissed my way back up her body and claimed her mouth, letting her taste herself on my lips.

"You're not done yet," I said, cock throbbing almost painfully against her thigh. I needed to bury myself inside her, to feel the pulse of her release around me.

She moaned, nails scoring down my back. "Take me, Cikarius. I'm yours."

Unable to resist any longer, I positioned myself above her, my painfully hard cock desperate for relief only Mia could provide. Other females had given me pleasure before, but Mia was different—she was the only one who made my entire being ache with longing. Once I plunged into her body, I knew everything would change; there would be no one else for me.

With a growl, I thrust into her welcoming heat and stilled, savoring the sensation of her silken walls enveloping me. Nothing had ever felt so right, as if I was made to be here, joined with her in body and soul.

I gazed down at her, wonder and possessiveness warring within me. She was beauty personified, a vision to inspire poets and bring men to their knees. And she was mine, if only for this moment. I would make it last.

Drawing back slowly, I pushed into her again, setting up a leisurely rhythm designed for maximum pleasure. Her breath caught on every stroke, soft cries urging me on. I leaned down to capture her mouth, swallowing each sweet sound as I made love to her with reverence.

She was my salvation, my light in the darkness. My Mia. I poured all the emotions swirling inside me into each kiss, each caress, each stroke, hoping she understood what I couldn't say. That she was mine, now and forever.

She arched into me, nails digging deeper. "Harder, Cikarius. I need more."

I increased my pace, hips snapping forward to bury myself to the hilt again and again. Her moans rose in pitch, inner walls fluttering around my length. I was close, so close, but I wouldn't find release until she came undone around me.

Reaching between us, I stroked her clit in time with my thrusts. Her back bowed off the ground as she shattered around me, a scream tearing from her throat. I followed after her, growling her name as I emptied myself inside her welcoming heat.

Collapsing beside her, I gathered her close. She curled into my embrace with a contented sigh, tracing idle patterns across my chest. I pressed a kiss to her hair, breathing in her scent.

"You're mine now. No one will ever take you from me."

My words held the weight of a vow. I would kill anyone who dared try to separate us, Sionagog Syndicate be damned. She was my mate, my heart, my everything.

Mia tilted her head up, lips curving into a soft smile. "And you're mine. Always."

Joy and possessiveness warred within me at her declaration. I sealed my claim with a searing kiss, losing myself in her taste. When our lips parted, I gazed into eyes glowing with love and hoped I would never be alone again. She was my light, my salvation, my home.

And I would destroy anything that threatened what was mine.

Before long, Mia's breathing changed to the soft, even breathing of slumber. As I watched Mia sleep peacefully in my arms, I couldn't help but marvel at her beauty and resilience. She had faced the horrors of Dufair with courage and determination, a testament to the strength that lay within her. But it was her vulnerability in my embrace that truly captivated me, stirring emotions within me I had never thought possible.

The reality of our situation weighed heavily on my conscience. The truth of my past as a hit man loomed like a dark cloud over our newfound intimacy. Would she still desire me if she knew what I had done? Could she ever forgive me for the lives I'd taken? Could I forgive myself? Until now, I'd thought every target deserved their fate.

With every passing moment, my resolve to protect her only grew stronger. We would face unimaginable dangers in our quest for to get off Dufair, but I was determined to stand by her side, no matter the cost.

"Sleep well, Mia," I whispered, pressing a gentle kiss to her forehead. She sighed contentedly in response, burrowing deeper into my arms.

As I held her close, an unfamiliar warmth spread through

my chest. Our attraction would be tested in the coming days, but there was nothing we couldn't overcome together.

"Whatever happens, I'll protect you," I said, my words barely audible even to my own ears. "I promise."

I carefully shifted my weight, trying not to disturb her as I pulled on my clothes. The darkness of the cave closed in around me, reflecting the uncertainty that lay ahead.

Gently, I reached into my pocket and pulled out the mission instructions, along with the photo of Mia that had been provided. My gaze lingered on her image, a reminder of the woman who had stolen my heart and given me something worth fighting for.

With a deep breath, I pulled out my communication tablet and composed a message to the Sionagog Syndicate. It was terse but clear: "I resign."

I hesitated for a moment before hitting send, knowing that there would be no turning back once the message hit my employer's inbox. The consequences of my decision weighed heavily on my mind. No one had ever left the Sionagog Syndicate before. What would happen now?

As I sent the message, both fear and determination coursed through me. Our path would be fraught with danger, but I was prepared to face it head-on to protect Mia.

In the cave's darkness, thoughts of the depth of my feelings for her consumed me, my protective instincts solidifying my commitment to her. Even if Mia never wanted to see me again, I would never stop protecting her. But now, I needed to find out who wanted her out of the way.

CHAPTER 5
MIA

woke in Cikarius's arms, heat pooling between my legs. The warmth of Cikarius's body spooned against mine, stirred that familiar heat deep inside me. His hard cock pressed into the small of my back, an insistent reminder of my insatiable desire for him. And I wanted him inside me again. How did this stranger ignite such passion in me?

Turning in his arms, I reached down, taking hold of his already hard cock. He groaned, his eyes darkening with lust. I slid my hand up to caress the marks on his chest, feeling the raised skin beneath my fingertips, wondering what secrets they held. But there was no time to ponder over it; our need for each other was overpowering. With a swift motion, he captured my hands and pinned me to the ground. His growl of desire sent shivers down my spine.

"Can't get enough, can you?" he asked, his breath hot against my ear. "We need to get moving. The slavers will be looking for us."

Desperate to feel alive despite the imminent danger, I arched up into Cikarius's cock. I've never had this kind of connection with anyone before. Never wanted someone so desperately. Every nerve ending in my body screamed for their touch.

"You'll think more clearly once you take care of that." I nodded to his crotch.

I itched to touch his chest, trace the marks there, but with my hands pinned I could do nothing. Why did he pull my hands away? Not that I minded. The thrill of being pinned under him fuelled my desire. Another thrust of my hips upward pulled a moan from Cikarius's lips. A smile of triumph curled my lips.

As he positioned himself over me, my thoughts drifted to the thought that Cikarius had saved me from the slavers, but now he seemed to be claiming me as his own. Was it really better this way? But the moment his fingers grazed my sensitive bud, all coherent thought evaporated. I gasped, arching my back as waves of pleasure threatened to overwhelm me.

"You're so wet for me already," Cikarius said, dipping a finger into my core.

I arched into his hand, wanting his cock to fill me instead. But I would take anything he wanted to give me.

"What are you going to do about it?" I asked.

A wicked grin turned his lips up and he thrust into me with unbridled passion, igniting a firestorm of pleasure that threatened to consume me entirely. Our bodies moved in perfect harmony, driven by an intensity neither of us had ever experienced before. Every nerve ending in my body was alight with sensations that left me breathless and begging for more.

"Harder," I begged, wrapping my legs around his hips, pulling him deeper inside me. I never begged, but with Cikarius, I needed his touch more than I needed to breathe.

Cikarius bent to capture my lips in a kiss, still thrusting into me. He drove into me harder and deeper and I undulated my hips into him, desperate for release. At some point,

Cikarius released my wrists, and I wrapped my arms around him, urging him to pump harder and faster.

A coil built inside me, eager to spring. It was a sensation like nothing I'd ever had before with anyone else. Each thrust brought me closer to the edge, closer to blissful oblivion. I moaned, my legs tightening around Cikarius's waist, urging him deeper.

At the first twitch of his orgasm, the wave of my climax crashed over me. He shuddered, spilling himself inside me. My walls clenched his cock, and I held him there, pulling every last drop out of him. Pulses ricocheted through me still, making every inch of my body sensitive to the touch.

When the orgasm finally abated, I sucked in a deep, shuddering breath.

He peered down at me. "And you were right. I can think much more clearly now." He grinned. "But now I want to do that again, and again, and again.

My heart fluttered, and I gulped. "I…want…that, too," I said, still struggling to catch my breath as we lay tangled together on the cave floor. "It's never been like that before."

"For me either," he said, his eyes filled with a rare vulnerability that made my heart swell with affection.

"Not even the glowing thing you did?"

He chuckled and shook his head. "That has never happened before."

"We just fit, you know?" Even as I said it, I knew it sounded lame.

But that was the only way I could describe it. There was none of the awkwardness that sex between strangers usually held. It was like we were attuned to each other's body, each other's needs. Meant for each other somehow. A ripple of fear skittered through me at the thought of never having this connection again.

Cikarius grinned again. "I do, in fact, know."

Heat suffused my cheeks. Of course, he knew. He was

here when all the fantastic sex was happening. I didn't imagine it or dream it. The sweet aches in my limbs told me every thrust, every moan, every caress had been as real as the luminescent plants I studied.

"Come on," Cikarius said, his voice gentle but firm. "We need to get moving. The slavers will be looking for us."

I sighed, content to remain here forever if it meant keeping him inside me - body and soul. But he was right; there would be time to explore this blossoming bond once we were safe from those who hunted us.

As we got dressed and started packing our belongings, I admired the way the light spilling into the cave played across Cikarius's sculpted form. His violet skin was even more alluring now, and I decided purple was my new favorite color.

Once clothed, I rifled through the contents of my pack. My samples and research were intact, thankfully, though I mourned the loss of my communicator. There was no way to contact the station or request emergency transport without it. We were on our own until we could find help.

I went through my computer and samples, ensuring that nothing important was lost. A sudden pang of sadness hit me as I thought of Amund. I couldn't let his death be in vain, and that meant being meticulous and methodical with my research.

As I delved deeper into the data and documents, a few disturbing documents caught my eye. Positive the missives were meant for someone else, I read them and gasped. They'd been left on a server that I had access to yet rarely used. Corporate espionage? I didn't have time to delve into it in depth, but I would get to the bottom of it.

"What's wrong?" Cikarius asked.

Warmth from the proximity of his body flooded me, creating a calming effect. I pointed to the screen on my laptop. "Corporate espionage."

"Of course," Cikarius said. "That explains why someone hired the slavers to get you."

I nodded, feeling a newfound determination to uncover the truth. As we delved deeper into the evidence, connecting the dots and piecing together the puzzle of the espionage, I couldn't help but marvel at how well Cikarius and I worked together. Despite our vastly different backgrounds and abilities, we shared an unbreakable connection that only grew stronger with each passing moment.

"To sentence me to a fate worse than death with the slavers? For what? Enhanced weapons?"

Deiridh Airm Solutions only had one rival on Alfataken Station. Maith Airm Weapons.

He leaned toward me, but didn't touch me. We both knew that would be dangerous. My body craved his touch again, and we couldn't afford to stay in the cave much longer.

"I won't let anyone hurt you."

"I believe you."

"We need to get moving," Cikarius said, his voice tinged with urgency.

I nodded in agreement. "You're right; we can't risk staying here any longer."

We quickly gathered our belongings and prepared to continue our journey. As I watched Cikarius effortlessly sling his pack over his shoulder, a newfound appreciation for his muscular form washed over me.

"Are you ready?" Cikarius asked, his voice pulling me from my reverie.

"Yes," I replied, my resolve strengthened by the task ahead. "Let's get off this moon."

Together, we emerged from the cave and ventured deeper into the treacherous jungle, determined to protect my research and ourselves from the ever-present dangers that lurked around every corner.

As we continued through the dense jungle, I felt a

growing sense of unease. The weight of our discoveries had taken its toll on both of us. Discovery of the corporate espionage and the implications it had for my work and my life consumed my thoughts.

The path ahead of us grew increasingly treacherous, and I clung to Cikarius as we navigated through the dense foliage. The sounds of unseen creatures surrounded us, their eerie calls a constant reminder of the danger lurking in the shadows.

As day turned into night, the jungle transformed before our eyes. The bioluminescent plants took center stage, casting a breathtaking glow that illuminated our surroundings. The beauty of the scene was almost surreal, yet the ever-present danger kept us on high alert.

"Maybe we should rest for a while," Cikarius suggested, noticing my growing exhaustion. We found a small alcove hidden among the trees, providing us with a temporary sanctuary from the perils of the jungle.

Cikarius's muscular arms enveloped me, pulling me close to his chest. Our bodies fit together perfectly, and I marveled at the intimate connection between us. Despite our dire circumstances, I felt an overwhelming sense of peace and security in his embrace.

It was too risky to do what I wanted to do with Cikarius, so I picked up my laptop and dove into the documents I'd found earlier. Denial still floated in my mind, unable to reconcile what I knew of my colleagues with the extent of the betrayal I suffered. And Amund had died for.

As we continued examining the evidence, a growing sense of unease settled in my shoulders. The full extent of the conspiracy and the danger I was in became increasingly clear. It wasn't just about my research anymore—it was about my life. I glanced at the luminescent flora samples in the backpack, their ethereal glow casting an eerie light across our makeshift workspace in the alcove. Their beauty and uniqueness were undeniable, but I couldn't ignore the potential for disaster if they fell into the wrong hands as advanced bioweapons.

"Can you imagine what they could do with these?" I asked Cikarius quietly, gesturing towards the glowing plants. "It's terrifying."

He nodded solemnly. "We have to protect your research, Mia. And you."

I paused, taking a moment to reflect on the implications of the espionage on my life's work and my safety. I had dedicated so much time and effort to my research, and now it was all in jeopardy. But I refused to let the fear consume me. I needed to stay strong, not just for myself, but for Cikarius, too.

"Maybe there's something we're missing," I murmured, returning to the computer screen. As I scrolled through files, searching for any hidden messages or clues, a sudden notification popped up. I clicked on it, only to be greeted by a threatening communication related to the espionage.

"Someone knows we're onto them," I whispered, feeling my heart race in my chest. "They're watching us. Or tracking my activity on the laptop somehow."

Cikarius's grip on my hand tightened, and his eyes blazed with protective fury. "We need to move. Now."

As we hastily gathered our belongings, preparing to flee the alcove, I wondered what dangers lay ahead. With enemies lurking in every shadow, it seemed that nowhere was truly safe. But one thing was certain: together, Cikarius and I would face whatever challenges awaited us, determined to protect each other and the research that had become so much more than just a job.

"Ready?" Cikarius asked, his voice steady despite the peril we were in.

I nodded, my resolve unwavering. "Let's do this."

My determination to protect not only my research but also

Cikarius and myself grew stronger. We were a team now, and I couldn't help but hope that our newfound connection would be enough to see us through the challenges that lay ahead.

"Let's go," Cikarius said, his voice filled with resolve. "We'll find a way off Dufair and get to the bottom of this."

"Stay close to me," Cikarius instructed as we ventured out of the alcove and back into the luminescent wilds of Dufair. The vibrant colors and sounds of the jungle assaulted my senses, but fear and excitement coursed through my veins, drowning out any hesitation I might have felt.

I glanced at Cikarius as we walked, watching the play of muscles under his tight-fitting clothes and the purposeful set of his jaw. He moved with a predatory grace I found mesmerizing, every step conveying coiled strength and decisiveness. Heat pooled low in my belly at the memory of that power held in check, unleashed at my urging. I blushed, looking away before he could notice my reaction. What was I thinking? Now was hardly the time for such distractions when our very lives were at stake.

"Where will we go?" I asked, trying to keep my voice steady despite the pounding of my heart.

"First, we need to contact Alfataken Station," he said, his yellow eyes scanning the dense foliage for threats. "We can't risk using conventional communication methods; they'll be monitoring those."

I nodded, understanding the gravity of the situation. The conspiracy that had targeted me went deeper than I had ever imagined, and exposing it would require careful planning and execution.

As we continued our journey through the jungle, I reflected on the connection Cikarius and I shared. It was unlike anything I had ever experienced, a bond forged in the heat of battle and solidified by the passion that had ignited between us. Despite the imminent danger, I couldn't help but feel a sense of belonging in his arms.

Our progress was slow but steady, with Cikarius expertly navigating the treacherous terrain. At one point, we stumbled upon a clearing filled with beautiful, glowing flora. Their delicate petals emitted an ethereal light, casting an other-worldly glow on everything they touched.

"Keep moving," Cikarius urged, yet his own gaze lingered on the exquisite sight for a moment longer than necessary.

"Are these the samples you were working on?" he asked, curiosity evident in his voice.

"Similar," I said. "These plants have the potential to revolutionize entire industries, but also to become powerful bioweapons if they fall into the wrong hands."

"Like Maith Airm Weapons?" he asked, his expression darkening at the mention of the rival corporation.

"Exactly," I confirmed. "Someone within my research team must have sold us out, and now they're after me and my work."

Cikarius's jaw clenched. "We'll figure all of this out and make sure your research is safe," he said.

The jungle seemed to close in, its shadows growing darker, as if echoing the danger we faced. But even amidst the chaos and fear, I found solace in Cikarius's presence. The connection between us had grown stronger still, and I couldn't deny the intensity of the feelings that pulled me toward him.

CHAPTER 6
MIA

The sharp chirp of Cikarius's device sliced through the humid air of Dufair's jungle moon, an unnatural sound amidst the symphony of nocturnal creatures. My gaze flickered to his hand, drawn by the urgency of that digital cry. He glanced at the screen, and I—driven by a compulsion I didn't fully understand—peered over his shoulder.

A picture flashed before my eyes. Me. But not the grainy image from the slavers' grim collection; this one was recent, detailed, chilling in its clarity. A fool—that's what I was, how I felt as blood turned to ice in my veins. My heart hammered against my ribcage, a frantic beat threatening to burst free.

He shoved the device in his pocket, guilt flashing in his eyes. "You weren't meant to see that."

How could I have been so blind? Every smile he had given me, every touch—I dissected them all now, searching for the lie beneath the surface. The way my name rolled off his tongue with a strange tenderness, was that just part of the act? The scent of his skin, a mix of the alien foliage and something uniquely him, had I imagined the comfort it brought?

In the luminescent glow of the jungle, dread crept over me

like the creeping vines on the jungle floor. The trust I'd extended to him, the warmth I'd allowed myself to feel in his presence—it crumbled, replaced by a sense of betrayal that twisted my stomach into knots.

"You did tell me you were dangerous."

An internal war raged within me, an onslaught of emotions battling for dominance. Confusion clouded my mind like the dense fog that hung over the luminescent wilds at dawn. Could I reconcile the man who had saved me with the one who might have orchestrated it all? My hands shook with the force of my inner tumult, fingers brushing against the cool metal of my field research kit—a reminder of the life I knew, the reality I trusted.

I sniffed, attempting to center myself, to find some semblance of the analytical calm that defined me. But even the familiar scents of damp soil and exotic flowers couldn't mask the acrid stink of deception that now permeated the surrounding air.

His hand reached out, a silent offering, but I recoiled. His touch had once sparked a current that ran deep, igniting sensations that left me breathless and hungry for more. Now, the thought filled me with an ache, a longing for something genuine that I feared had never been real.

I closed my eyes, trying to steady my racing pulse, to shut out the vibrant world that suddenly felt like a façade. When I opened them again, it was to the sight of his glowing yellow eyes, watching me with an intensity that made my skin prickle with both anticipation and dread.

His expression wavered, hinting at an emotion I couldn't quite place. Was it regret? Or simply the calculation of a being whose very existence was predicated on deception?

The silence stretched on, thick as the undergrowth that surrounded us, until I couldn't stand it any longer. I had to move, to flee from the truth that threatened to engulf me.

And so, I ran, darting past him into the unknown depths

of the jungle, each step propelling me forward but no closer to understanding the enigma that was Cikarius. As the underbrush clawed at my clothes and skin, a single thought echoed through the cacophony of fear and desire that consumed me:

Could I survive the night?

I stumbled through the underbrush, my breaths coming out in ragged gasps. The luminescent leaves cast eerie shadows on the ground, and every snap of a twig underfoot sent jolts of panic up my spine.

"Mia, stop." Cikarius's voice cut through the dense foliage, a low rumble that sounded both commanding and desperate.

I paused, heart hammering, chest heaving. His words carried weight, an anchor in the storm of my thoughts. It didn't surprise me that he could catch up to me so quickly. I turned to face him, his silhouette framed by the otherworldly glow of Dufair's nocturnal flora.

"Can I trust you?" The question finally broke free, laced with vulnerability.

His gaze never wavered as he took a step closer. "Yes."

"You weren't in that area of the jungle randomly." The statement wasn't a question; I knew it, he knew it.

"No."

"Rumors from Alfataken Station…" My voice trailed off, the memory of whispered tales sending a shiver down my spine.

Cikarius closed the distance between us, each step measured. He stopped just a breath away, close enough that I could see the faint gleam of those marks on his chest, scars from a life I couldn't comprehend.

"Every mission given to me, I've completed," he said, the glow from the plants casting his purple skin in haunting hues.

"Every person you killed," I corrected, bile rising in my throat.

He nodded, and for a moment, I saw a flicker of something resembling pain flash across his features.

"Everything changed when I saw you," he said, voice barely above a whisper. "I had to save you."

"And claim me?" My voice was a tremulous whisper, betraying the turmoil within.

"Yes," he admitted. "But we, the Marbhadh, we're not supposed to feel that. Our fated mate is engineered out of us. We're only meant to kill."

The revelation hung heavy in the air, mingling with the scents of damp soil and alien blooms. A part of me longed to reach out, to bridge the gap between us, but fear rooted me to the spot.

"Then what am I to you?" I asked, the question tearing at my very soul.

"You are the exception," he said, closing the last bit of space between us until his warmth enveloped me. "My anomaly."

"Every girl loves to be called an anomaly."

"Mia, you are everything to me. My fated mate. I knew it the moment I claimed you and my skin glowed with each touch."

In that moment, the jungle seemed to hold its breath, the usual cacophony silenced by the gravity of his admission. His touch was gentle, a contrast to the strength and savagery I knew lay just beneath the surface.

Could I trust a creature designed to kill? Was the pull I felt towards him part of some grand design or simply the chaos of an uncharted heart?

As Cikarius's arms encircled me, a protective cocoon in the wilds of Dufair, I realized I might never have the answers. But as I leaned into his embrace, feeling the steady beat of his heart against mine, I decided that, for now, it was enough.

Cikarius stood motionless, his yellow eyes fixed on me,

waiting. My heart pounded a frantic rhythm, threatening to betray the fear I fought to contain.

"You could have killed me. Any time," I said, my voice quivering as I spoke, the list of moments flashing through my mind. "When the slavers caught me, when we crossed the laghairt, in the cave, even now."

"Yet here you stand," he said, his tone steady but not unkind.

"It's true then? You're a hit man?"

"Resigned," he said, as if tasting the word, letting it roll off his tongue. He nodded slowly. "For you."

My mind reeled. Could such a thing be possible? A genetically engineered assassin, defying his own creation for... what? For me?

"Is that even possible?" I pressed, searching his face for any hint of deception.

"I don't know. No one else has ever tried." His shoulders tensed, the glowing marks across his chest visible even in the dim light from the bioluminescent moss clinging to the trees.

I looked up to see the conflict etched into the lines of his stoic face. It was a vulnerability I hadn't expected from someone so formidable.

"Every instinct in me is engineered for killing," he said, "but none of that matters anymore. Not since I found you."

"Then show me," I said, my voice barely audible above the hum of the jungle. "Show me I'm more to you than just another mission."

His arms tightened around me, not with possession but with promise. He pulled away, clasped my hand, and led me deeper into the shadows of the jungle.

For the first time since I'd met Cikarius, I wasn't thinking about tomorrow. Only the heat of his body against mine and the shared heartbeat that echoed our mutual resolve.

Unable to continue, I pulled my hand from his. Too many questions, too many reservations swirled in my head. The bioluminescent glow from the moss cast eerie shadows across Cikarius's face, his yellow eyes reflecting the light like some nocturnal predator. My mind was a maelstrom, swirling with the desperate desire to trust him, to lean into the warmth of his presence, and the icy dread that he might still be what he was created to be—a killer.

"Can I really believe you won't turn on me?" I said, my voice barely rising above the sound of our synchronized breathing. "Your genetics, they were designed for one purpose."

Cikarius stood motionless, a statue carved from the very darkness that threatened to consume us both. His silence weighed heavily between us, and I felt the chasm of doubt widen.

"When I look at you, I don't see the assassin," I said, my gaze fixed on the undulating shadows that played across his muscular frame. "But it's there, isn't it? Part of you?"

My throat constricted around the next words, confessing more than just fear. "I can't help but want you, even though part of me is terrified that one day…you might fulfill your mission. And that mission could be me."

The intensity in his gaze never wavered, yet something shifted within those fathomless eyes—a flicker of something human, something kindred. My chest tightened at the vulnerability that bled through the cracks of his façade, my own defenses threatening to crumble.

"Every moment I am with you, Cikarius, I'm fighting myself. Fighting the instinct that says you're my soulmate against the fear that it's all just a prelude to my end." My fingers grazed the cool metal of the pendant around my neck, a present from my mother before she died, a tangible reminder of the life I clung to.

He reached out slowly, his large hand enveloping mine with a gentleness that belied his strength. Warmth spread from his touch, seeping into the icy tendrils of fear that wrapped around my heart. His gesture, so full of intent and care, spoke louder than any reassurance could have.

"Please, I need to know," I said, my voice trailing off as if the rest of my plea hung suspended in the charged air between us.

His hand tightened around mine, anchoring me to the present, to him, to the possibility that maybe, just maybe, we could transcend the past that haunted us both. His other hand rose, fingertips grazing my cheek with a tenderness that made my knees weaken. The simple touch was electric, sending shivers down my spine, awakening a yearning that I had no right to feel—not now, not when danger lurked within him.

I drew in a shaky breath, my resolve teetering on the edge. Would I choose to step back into the safety of solitude, or would I fall into the unknown, into him?

A distant howl echoed through the jungle, a reminder of the perils that awaited us beyond this brief respite. My pulse quickened, my decision hanging in the balance as the night closed in around us.

"Your fear… it's a scent on the wind, Mia," Cikarius said, his voice a melodic rumble. "But I swear on every star in this system, your safety is my commandment, one I would die to uphold."

His declaration hung heavy in the damp air of the jungle, as substantial and tactile as the bioluminescent moss beneath our feet. My chest tightened with the weight of his words; they were an anchor in a storm, promising salvation amidst tempestuous doubts.

"I don't know what a soulmate is," he said, his glowing yellow gaze piercing through the shadows, latching onto mine with an intensity that felt like a physical force. "If it means a fated mate… then yes, you are mine, Mia Clarke. And I am bound to you, beyond genetics, beyond any mission I was engineered to complete."

I swallowed hard, the lump in my throat making it difficult to speak. My instincts screamed at me to flee, to survive, but something primal within me whispered that survival might lie in the embrace of the danger before me.

"Can I truly trust you?" The question escaped my lips before I could stop it, a vulnerable admission that laid bare my inner turmoil for him to see. It wasn't just about trusting him—it was about trusting myself to make the right choice.

Cikarius's hand cradled my jaw with a gentleness that belied his strength. His thumb brushed against my lower lip, sending a thrill through me that was both exhilarating and terrifying.

"Trust is not given lightly," he said, his words vibrating through me. "It is earned, moment by moment. Let me earn yours, Mia."

I was caught in the gravity of his gaze, his presence, his inexplicable sincerity. A shimmering cocoon seemed to form around us, isolating us from the rest of existence. In that suspended reality, my guard lowered, inch by precarious inch. The hardness that had armored my heart softened, molten by the warmth emanating from his skin.

"Maybe..." I started, my voice barely a whisper, "maybe I can learn to trust again."

The corner of his mouth lifted in a ghost of a smile, offering a glimpse of the man who might exist beyond the assassin, the protector. His touch lingered, branding me with the promise of what could be if we dared to explore the connection that drew us inexplicably together.

His hand slid from my face to the nape of my neck, drawing me closer. The space between us closed, and I could feel the steady rhythm of his heart against mine. His touch was gentle, almost reverent, as if he recognized the fragility of the trust that weaved between us.

In the cocoon of his arms, the world outside faded into insignificance. The dangers lurking in the jungle's shadows, the labyrinthine politics of Alfataken Station, even the haunting secrets of Talamhmar—all paled in comparison to the immediacy of his embrace.

I tilted my head back, looking up at him, searching his glowing eyes for the truth I so desperately needed. There, in the depths of his gaze, I found something that transcended fear, something pure and unwavering. It was protection, it was promise—it was the assurance that he would stand between me and any threat, no matter the cost.

"Stay with me," he said, his voice a low rumble that resonated through my core. "Let me keep you safe."

CHAPTER 7
CIKARIUS

waited, the air between us charged with unspoken tension. The jungle's cacophony faded into the background as I watched Mia process the reality of her situation, my revelation hovering over us like a specter. Her life was in the crosshairs because of me, and the weight of that truth bore down on my shoulders with an intensity I hadn't anticipated.

"Will you let me protect you?" I asked, my voice low, barely a whisper against the din of Dufair's nightlife. I needed her to say yes, not only for her safety but for the sanity that was slipping through my fingers like grains of sand. The Sionagog Syndicate wouldn't let go easily; they were as much a part of me as my own flesh and blood—a flesh engineered for one purpose.

Mia's eyes held mine, green pools reflecting a depth of emotion that made my heart clench. She didn't know the battle raging inside me, the war between the cold assassin I was created to be and the man, no, the creature, yearning to break free from those chains. A creature who now stood at the precipice of change because of her.

"Even if you decide to leave, I will follow," I said, the

confession scraping against my insides. Acknowledging it felt like defeat and victory all at once. Carelessness had led her to see the message, my orders to eliminate her—orders I could no longer obey.

Mia's gaze never wavered. "You were sent to kill me…"

"Was," I emphasized the word, allowing the past tense to hang between us. "Now, I'm choosing to defy them. For you." It sounded like a vow, and perhaps it was—the first one I'd ever made of my own volition.

"Can a weapon really forsake its nature?" she asked, her words a caress against the harsh truth we faced.

"Perhaps not," I admitted, feeling the predator stir within me. "But this weapon is yours now, if you'll have it."

A slow nod. Consent given. Relief flooded through me, though the taste of danger lingered on my tongue, a reminder of the precarious edge we balanced upon.

Her shoulders, previously tense as coiled vines, slumped in resignation. "I'll stay with you," she said, her voice a whisper that barely rose above the sighs of the wind through the luminescent leaves. "At least until we're off Dufair and back on Alfataken Station."

The words were a salve to the raw edges of my conscience. She would stay. And in her eyes—an emerald sea reflecting the moon's glow—I read not just acquiescence, but the beginnings of trust reborn. Affection simmered there, a promise of warmth in the cold expanse that had become my existence.

"Then we need to move," I said, pulling her gently by the arm. "The slavers will still be searching for you. We must reach the landing hub to find transport."

We ducked under hanging ferns, their fronds glowing like ghostly fingers. The air was thick, redolent with the scent of soil and the distant tang of rain waiting to fall.

"Your vehicle—can't we use it?" Mia's question cut through the cacophony of nocturnal creatures stirring in the underbrush.

I shook my head. "It's compromised. Since resigning from the Sionagog Syndicate, I can't trust it hasn't been sabotaged." My admission hung between us; an unsaid understanding that the odds were against us—that we were vulnerable in ways we couldn't afford to be.

With every step, the jungle closed in, a living entity aware of our plight, its whispers a siren song of both beauty and danger. But the determination in Mia's stride told me she had no intention of succumbing to fear, nor the darkness that sought to claim us.

Her eyes widened at my words, a flicker of fear—or maybe understanding—passing through them. "So, any sabotage would be subtle, not detonating until you're clear of civilians?" Mia's voice was calm, but the tension in her body betrayed her.

"Exactly," I said. "The Sionagog Syndicate isn't fond of unnecessary casualties. They draw unwanted attention." The surrounding jungle seemed to lean in, listening.

"And you work for them," she stated with an edge that cut deeper than any blade I'd wielded.

"Worked," I corrected sharply, feeling that familiar clench in my chest. "I was genetically engineered to be what they needed—a killer. But it's not a leash I wear willingly anymore." I took a step closer, the bioluminescent glow of the foliage painting us both in an ethereal light. "And I'm ready to leave that behind for you."

Mia remained silent, hoisting her backpack with trembling hands.

"Stay close," I said. "Do exactly as I say, without question."

"Understood," she said, her voice steady despite the fluster I had seen moments before.

I led the way, my senses heightened to every sound—the distant call of night predators, the rustle of leaves that may or may not have been just the wind. The moist soil beneath our feet left traces of our passage, and my mind raced with strategies to evade those who might be tracking us.

The air was heavy with the scent of fermenting fruit and wet foliage, sounds of nocturnal creatures punctuating the silence between us. My hand brushed against hers, a current running through us that felt like a surge of electricity, grounding yet volatile. It was a distraction, one we could ill afford, but it was also a reminder—of what was at stake, and what I was fighting for.

I kept my pace measured, ensuring Mia was always within arm's reach. There was comfort in knowing she was there, a strange warmth accompanying the concern that knotted my insides. I thought back to the cave, to the union of two unlikely souls seeking solace in each other's arms. The memory was vivid, visceral, almost enough to make me forget the peril that hunted us.

"Can we trust anyone on Alfataken Station?" Mia's voice, soft yet clear, pulled me from my reverie.

"Few," I said. "But I have contacts that owe me favors. We'll find safe passage off Dufair."

A sudden crackle of branches underfoot froze me in place. Instinctively, I reached back, pressing a finger to my lips to signal silence. Mia's eyes, wide with alarm, met mine as I pointed to the dense thicket behind a massive tree trunk. We slipped into the foliage, our bodies brushing against each other in the tight space, her breath shallow and quick against the side of my face.

The jungle's chorus fell silent under the heavy tread of boots, the slavers' voices closing in, slicing through the thick air. "She can't be far," one barked, his words sending a shiver down my spine—not from fear, but from the proximity of Mia. Her soft curves pressed against my hardened form. In that cramped hiding spot, every shift, every gasp, was an intimate dance of survival.

"Check over there!" another commanded. The slavers

were on top of us now, their shadows flitting across the foliage like specters hunting prey. Mia's trembling hand found the crook of my arm, her fingers gripping me tightly. The scent of her fear mingled with the primal tang of the jungle, strangely intoxicating.

Her heartbeat raced against my own, a drumbeat in sync with the danger that loomed mere breaths away. It was a perilous tango, our bodies moving together without music, only the pulse of our shared adrenaline. Her chest rose and fell rapidly against mine, and I fought the urge to pull her even closer, to shield her completely with my body.

"Nothing here," a voice grunted, frustration evident. The footsteps receded, the tension slowly unwinding from the air like a released spring. But we remained still, statues in a garden of shadows and moonlight, waiting for the threat to vanish entirely.

As the sounds of pursuit faded, replaced once again by the nocturnal symphony of Dufair, Mia shifted beside me, her movement sending fresh waves of awareness coursing through my veins. The brush of her body was a siren call to a part of me that yearned for more than just protection, more than duty—a yearning that was both human and something else entirely.

"Are they gone?" she whispered, her voice a caress that stirred the depths of my being.

"Wait," I said, every sense straining for signs of deception. The predator within me raged against the stillness, eager to claim what was so agonizingly close. Dispatch the slavers, thin their numbers.

But this wasn't about the hunt or the kill. It was about her—Mia, my mission, my fated mate. For her, I would defy my very nature; for her, I would become the protector instead of the assassin.

We waited, our breaths mingling, our futures hanging in the balance.

I grudgingly disentangled myself from the underbrush, muscles tensing with the effort to maintain distance from Mia. My body ached with a primal need, every fiber of my being protesting as I edged away from her warmth. The cool night air hit my skin, a stark contrast to the heat that had built between us.

"Stay here," I said, my voice a low rumble that vibrated in the charged silence. I slipped out of our hiding place, moving with the silence of a specter among the towering trees and luminescent foliage. The slavers' careless tracks marred the soft soil, leading away into the depths of the jungle. They wouldn't double back—not this time.

Returning to Mia, I reached for her hand, guiding her out with an assurance I didn't entirely feel. Her fingers brushed against mine, igniting something deep within me. She stumbled slightly, and instinctively, I caught her, pulling her close. Her body pressed against mine, a momentary lapse in discipline that sent a surge of longing through my veins.

"Sorry," she said, her eyes lifting to meet mine, reflecting a myriad of unspoken thoughts.

I released her more abruptly than intended. "We go left. It's safer."

After over an hour of hiking, an abandoned research facility loomed ahead, a relic of ambition now surrendered to decay. Its dilapidated walls stood defiant against the encroaching wilderness, a testament to forgotten projects and forsaken dreams. Flickering lights danced like ghosts along the corroded metal structures, casting eerie shadows that seemed to move of their own volition.

"Keep close," I said, as we approached the entrance, the scent of mold and stagnation greeting us like an unwelcome host. A creaking sign, half-illuminated, sputtered the name of the facility. Once proud, now it was nothing but a faded echo of its past glory.

We stepped inside, our footsteps echoing in the vast

emptiness. The air was stale, heavy with the weight of years untouched by living breath. Distant water dripped rhythmically, the sound amplified by the silence, a reminder that even in abandonment, life persisted.

"Watch your step," I advised, as Mia's foot found a weak floorboard, its groan piercing the quiet like a scream. She nodded, her eyes scanning the darkness as she sidestepped the hazard.

"Any idea what they researched here?" she asked, her voice barely above a whisper.

"Doesn't matter now," I said, though curiosity flared briefly within me. What secrets did these crumbling walls hide?

A sudden noise—a skittering in the darkness—halted us. We froze, two statues once again, listening for the threat that might lurk around any corner. My hand instinctively went to the weapon at my side, comforted by the familiar weight.

"Probably just some creature," Mia ventured, her tone betraying a hint of fear despite her scientific mind.

"Perhaps," I said, though I trusted nothing on this forsaken moon. My eyes adjusted to the dimness, seeking the source of the sound, ready to defend, to kill if necessary.

"Let's find somewhere defensible," I said, steering us toward what looked like a control center, its door hanging precariously off its hinges.

We entered, and I scanned the room, noting exits and potential threats. The dust lay thick, undisturbed, save for the footprints we now added to the floor's grim canvas.

"Here." I gestured to a corner with a clear view of the entrance. "We'll stay here until dawn."

Mia nodded, setting down her computer and samples carefully, as if they were the most precious cargo. And to her, they were—a lifeline to a world beyond this chaos.

"Thank you," she said, her eyes meeting mine. In them, I

saw gratitude, trust, and something else—a spark that mirrored my own desires.

"Always," I assured her. For Mia, I would withstand any temptation, confront any foe, defy my very creators. Because she was worth it—worth everything.

And as the distant howls of nocturnal predators pierced the stillness, I knew our respite would be brief. Danger was ever-present on Dufair, and the Sionagog Syndicate's shadow loomed large over us both. But for now, amid the flickering light and the promise of safety, I allowed myself one simple truth: I would protect Mia Clarke with my life.

Silence became a deceptive blanket, muffling the slow decay around us. Mia's breaths were even; her presence, a warm contrast to the cold sterility of our hideout. I watched over her, tuned to the slightest deviation in the jungle's nocturnal symphony.

Abruptly, the stillness cracked like brittle bone.

"Stay behind me," I said without turning, my senses flaring wide open as a figure emerged from the shadows. Varek Sorn filled the doorway, the Sionagog Syndicate's insignia glinting on his chest. His lithe frame coiled with tension, his gaze sharp and predatory.

"Congratulations, Cikarius," he said, his voice smooth as the silencer on a plasma rifle. "You've played the protector quite convincingly."

I stepped forward, placing myself between Mia and the operative. "She has nothing you want."

"Ah, but that's where you're wrong." A cruel smile played across Varek's thin lips. "The Sionagog Syndicate appreciates your… initiative. Complete your mission, prove your loyalty, and all is forgiven."

His words hung in the air, laced with an unspoken threat that chilled my blood. My fists clenched at my sides. Loyalty. That concept had become a jagged shard in my mind ever since Mia entered my life.

To rejoin the Syndicate… the idea swirled inside me like a toxic mist. No one walked away from the Syndicate and lived. The chase would never end; they would hunt me to the edge of the universe if necessary. Worse still, they could use Mia against me—a pawn in their merciless game. The mere thought tightened my chest, a rare sensation of dread wrapping around my heart.

I couldn't betray myself, not now. Not for the false promise of safety within the ranks of those who saw me as nothing more than a weapon. The jungle's humidity seeped into the facility, the air thick against my skin. I could almost taste the emerald leaves and the intoxicating flowers from the outside, a cruel reminder of the freedom just out of reach.

Varek watched me, his predatory eyes gleaming in anticipation. He smelled victory, but what he didn't know was that I smelled something too—the subtle perfume of Mia's fear mingling with the metallic tang of my resolve.

"Weigh your options carefully, Cikarius. You know what happens to those who cross us," he said, his voice dripping with dark honey.

I turned my head enough to glimpse Mia behind me. Her breaths shallow whispers in the heavy silence that fell over the facility.

I shifted, feeling the ground's grit against my boots, each granule a witness to this dance of death and deceit. Behind me, Mia's breath caught—a silent gasp that brushed my senses like the whisper of silk against skin. Her presence was a heat at my back, a beacon of life amidst the desolation. She tensed, her fear a palpable force that seemed to draw the darkness tighter around us.

"Your move, Cikarius," Varek coaxed, his voice soft as the brush of fur against flesh.

My heart hammered in my chest, a drumbeat calling me to war—a war within my very soul. I could feel the pulse of Dufair's luminescent jungle in my veins, its wildness a mirror

to my own. The Sionagog Syndicate was a shackle I had shattered, but now its links threatened to ensnare me once more.

"Time is not your ally," Varek said, mistaking my silence
for hesitation.

The faint glow of bioluminescent mold on the door cast
eerie shadows on his face, turning his confident smirk into a
ghoulish grin. He believed he held all the cards, that my next
move was already his to claim.

But he was wrong.

"Understood," I said, my voice a guttural affirmation of
my path. It was a lie cloaked in the garb of truth, a deception
born of necessity.

Mia's body quivered behind me, a bowstring drawn taut
with dread. She thought she knew what came next—that her
end was written in the stars above Talamhmar. But stars,
much like fate, were not as fixed as they seemed.

"Then do it," Varek whispered, each word a silken thread
weaving the web of my supposed destiny. "The mission
comes first."

In the stillness, I turned towards Mia, my movements
deliberate, betraying none of the storm that raged beneath my
calm exterior. Every step was a note in the symphony of our
entwined lives, a crescendo building towards an unknown
finale.

I turned back to Varek.

Varek's smile stretched across his face, a predator baring
its fangs, assured of the meal to come. He saw only what he
wanted to see: the last act of a play he thought he directed.

And as the scent of fear and determination mingled in the
air, I made my choice. "You're right. The mission does come
first."

CHAPTER 8
MIA

stood there, my heart racing with the kind of betrayal that seeps into your bones. "How can you say that?" I said, the words a thorn in my throat. Across the room, Varek's laughter skittered across my skin like ice, his mocking tones echoing off the cold metal walls of the lab. I moved to stand beside Cikarius, heat searing my cheeks as I looked him in the eyes.

"Because the mission always comes first." The voice, once warm and protective, now felt as alien to me as the jungle moon's glowing flora. Cikarius, the man who'd saved me from slavers, whose embrace had promised safety, was just another hit man. My mind reeled, but survival instincts kicked in—I needed a weapon, an escape, anything. But Varek was blocking the door, his slim figure a barrier as insurmountable as Alfataken station's hull.

Before I could move, Cikarius's muscular arms ensnared me, trapping me with ease. He positioned himself between me and Varek again, a living shield with a vice-like grip. Confusion mingled with the panic pounding through my veins, each heartbeat screaming for me to flee.

In the background, Varek's chuckle unfurled again, a

smug sound that filled the entire space. "Cikarius is the Sion-agog Syndicate's best assassin," he said, and I could almost feel the smugness radiating from him. "Always gets his man… or in this case, woman."

I fought against Cikarius's hold, muscles straining, skin slick with perspiration. The air tasted metallic, heavy with fear and the tang of impending violence. Around us, the lab was silent, save for the distant hum of lights and our own ragged breaths—a stark contrast to the vibrant cacophony of Dufair's jungles outside.

I couldn't believe it. This man, whose touch had ignited something primal within me, was now my captor. His scent, once a heady mix that pulled at my senses, now filled me with dread. But there was something in his eyes, a glint that didn't match the hard set of his jaw. It was almost like… No, I couldn't afford to hope. Not now.

My heart hammered against my ribcage, a frantic drum-beat in the lab's silence. The air was electric with tension, every instinct screaming at me to flee, but Cikarius's iron grip held me fast. How could I have fallen so hard for his façade? I mentally chastised myself for being such a fool, even as I felt the ripple of his muscles tighten around me.

"Hide when I say," he whispered into my ear, his voice a low thrum that sent shivers down my spine despite the danger. Confusion clouded my thoughts, his words a puzzle I couldn't solve amidst the chaos.

"Why—" I started, but his eyes cut me off, their yellow glow fierce and unyielding.

"Understand?" His question was a command, and I nodded, more lost than ever.

"Get on with it," Varek's voice sliced through the thick atmosphere, impatient, cold. "We have news for Ivor."

The mention of Ivor sparked a fire in my belly. My mind raced, piecing together fragments of information, trying to make sense of the madness.

"Ivor Arteus?" The name slipped from my lips before I could catch it, a gasp that betrayed the shock constricting my throat. Ivor—calm, collected Ivor, with his sharp suits and sharper business acumen—intertwined in this web of deceit? It was incomprehensible.

"He's my boss's competition," I said, my voice barely above a whisper, the words tasting like betrayal. "He owns the only other firearms company worth mentioning on Alfataken Station." Memories of formal dinners and polite conversation swirled in my head, now tainted with the sour sting of treachery. Ivor killing for profit? It was a chilling thought.

"Enough of the chatter." Varek's command was a whip-crack in the stillness, his intent clear as the sterile light that bathed us all in its unforgiving glow.

Cikarius's response came smooth as silk, a deadly promise. "Gladly."

His next words were for me alone, a secret shared in the barest of whispers, a brush of his lips against the shell of my ear sending involuntary shivers down my spine. "Now."

With those words, he spun around, and I knew this was the moment to act. His declaration hung in the air, heavy with meaning. "The mission is Mia's safety and happiness."

A flood of adrenaline surged through me at his signal, my legs carrying me away with a haste born of survival instinct. I darted toward the cover of the counters, my mind reeling at Cikarius's allegiance. Was this another deception, or had the assassin with eyes like molten gold truly turned against his orders for me?

As I crouched low, hidden from view, I couldn't help but glance over my shoulder. Cikarius faced Varek, the tension between them palpable. And then it began—a dance of lethal intent—as Cikarius moved with a grace that belied his size, each motion deliberate, each strike a silent vow of protection.

My breath caught, time slowing as the two men circled,

predators locked in a battle where only one could prevail. Every fiber of my being urged me to run, yet I stayed frozen, watching, waiting, knowing that my life hung in the balance of this violent ballet.

"Only two will walk out of here," Cikarius's words echoed in my mind, a grim prophecy as I watched him fight for both our futures.

I flinched as another blow landed, the sound of flesh on flesh echoing through the abandoned facility. Cikarius was a symphony of violence, each move a deadly note played out before me. Varek's eyes, once so sure, now flickered with fear as he struggled to counter the relentless assault.

The air was thick with the metallic tang of blood and sweat. My heart hammered against my ribs, an erratic drumbeat syncing with the cadence of their combat. I could feel every strike in my bones, a jarring dance of death that both terrified and mesmerized me.

"Should've known better than to stand against me," Varek spat between gasps for breath, his voice a razor sliding across my nerves. He parried a punch, then twisted, his heel grazing Cikarius's temple. A temporary reprieve, but it was clear—he could match Cikarius's skills.

My stomach knotted at the thought. If Varek won, I'd be next. His promise to complete Cikarius's original mission—to end my life—hung in the air, heavy and suffocating. But the threat didn't stop there. "And once you're gone, traitor, they'll pay handsomely for your head, too."

Dust and debris rose like ghosts around them as they circled one another, two predators locked in a lethal waltz. The facility groaned around us, a lament for the violence it sheltered.

I could sense the shift in Cikarius, the tension in his shoulders coiling tighter than the springs in the derelict machinery that surrounded us. His gaze fixed on Varek, a silent vow that he wouldn't let harm come to me.

Their dance continued, a blur of movement and fury. My senses were overwhelmed—the stench of oil, the cold bite of the metal floor beneath me, the electric hum of the flickering lights.

As they fought, my mind raced. We needed to escape, to get to Ivor's base and alert authorities about the corporate espionage—but first, we had to survive this fight.

Cikarius's fist connected with a sickening crunch, and Varek stumbled back. For a moment, time seemed to slow, and I saw the outcome written in the stark lines of determination etched on Cikarius's face.

"Never going to happen," Cikarius said, each syllable a promise as deadly as the blows he dealt. "Only two of us will leave this lab." His words cut through the cacophony of our desperate struggle, and I watched, heart thudding against my ribs, as Varek's smugness crumbled beneath the weight of Cikarius's resolve.

Varek was formidable—another creation of twisted science like Cikarius—but there was something in Cikarius's eyes, a blazing fury that wouldn't be quenched. My breath caught in my throat, the air heavy with the tang of heated metal and the electric scent of fear.

They clashed, a symphony of violence played out in grunts and the harsh ring of flesh on flesh. Every nerve ending screamed for me to look away, but I couldn't. Not when Cikarius fought for more than survival—for loyalty, for a bond that defied his very design.

A final crushing blow, and Varek's body crumpled to the ground, lifeless. The sound echoed in the empty space, a stark reminder of the line Cikarius had crossed for me. For us.

My pulse hammered, a frenzied rhythm that mirrored the chaos of my emotions. Gratitude, terror, and an inexplicable warmth swirled within me as I edged from behind the counter. The metallic tang of blood filled my mouth, its iron grip a contrast to the soft give of moss underfoot as I moved closer to him.

"Thank you," I said, the words scraping raw from my throat. Trembling fingers reached out, brushing against the cool, purple skin of his arm. It was an anchor in the storm, the solid reality of his presence pulling me back from the precipice of panic.

His arms enveloped me then, a fortress of muscle and sinew that shielded me from the world. In that embrace, the chill of the abandoned facility melted away, replaced by the heat radiating from his body. I shivered, not from the cold but from the sudden, searing awareness of every point where our bodies touched.

"Safe," he said, and the single word was a benediction, a vow that resonated deep in my bones. The danger wasn't over; far from it. But in that moment, held close by the assassin who'd sworn to protect me, I allowed myself the luxury of believing it could be true.

As we stood among the remnants of what had been a fight for life, a new battle loomed on the horizon. With Varek's still form at our feet, a chilling prelude to what awaited us outside, I knew that whatever came next; we were a team.

And as we turned to leave the dim glow of the research facility behind, I couldn't shake the feeling that despite the respite of Cikarius's arms, the darkness of Dufair's jungles harbored threats far greater than any we had yet encountered.

The cold seeped into my bones as I watched Cikarius close the eyes of the man he had just killed. The lab, once a hub of innovation and discovery, now felt like a tomb, silent except for the hum of abandoned machinery. Cikarius's jaw was set, his yellow eyes fixed on some distant point only he could see.

"We need to move," he said, his voice slicing through the stillness.

I nodded, the weight of what lay ahead settling in my stomach like a stone. Ivor's base—a den of corporate espionage so entwined with power that it seemed invincible. But we had to try; the evidence we'd gathered was too damning to ignore.

"Let's go then. I need to find a computer, one with more power than my laptop."

Cikarius nodded. "Be quick about it. I don't want to hang around here too long."

CHAPTER 9
CIKARIUS

Leaning against cold metal, I watched Mia from the doorway, the flicker of holographic displays casting an ethereal light on her concentrated face. Mia's fingers danced over the keyboard with a grace that belied their speed, her green eyes reflecting the determined spirit that had drawn me to her—that and something else, a tenderness I hadn't known I was capable of feeling.

The room hummed with the dormant technology of the abandoned facility, now buzzing back to life under her command. The scent of ionized air mingled with the mustiness of disuse, creating a unique fragrance marking this moment—her brilliance awakening the slumbering beast of machinery.

"Damn it," she said, her voice barely audible over the whir of reactivated systems. "Not enough processing power."

She stood, surveying the banks of ancient computers, her ponytail swaying as she scanned for a solution. I admired her tenacity, the meticulous way she approached each obstacle, so different from my own brute-force tactics. I stepped into the room, feeling the weight of my past actions, the ease with which I had taken lives. It was a stark contrast to the life I now vowed to protect.

"Let me try the mainframe," I said, moving towards the bulky computer terminals lining the opposite wall. I didn't understand the pull I felt towards her, this human woman whose life had become intertwined with mine in a dance of fate and survival.

Mia nodded, acceptance mingling with a flicker of approval in her green eyes. I reached the terminal, my fingers more accustomed to triggers than keyboards, but I adapted. Adaptation was survival, after all.

With a few expert commands, Mia awakened the dormant system, its screens flickering to life like bioluminescent leaves in Dufair's twilight. Together, we dove into the labyrinth of data, searching for the threads that would unravel Ivor's schemes.

"Here," Mia said, pointing at a complex diagram that sprawled across the screen like a digital spiderweb. "Look at these transactions."

"Shell companies." My voice was flat, a stark contrast to the crackle of energy that surged through the room as we pieced together the puzzle of betrayal and deceit.

"Exactly. Ivor's been funneling funds for years, but what for?" Her question hung in the air, laced with the scent of ozone.

We worked in tandem, our movements synchronized in a silent dance of discovery. Every so often, Mia's hand brushed against mine, sending jolts of electricity through my body, igniting something within that no amount of genetic engineering could have predicted.

"Got something," I finally announced, a cluster of encrypted files yielding to Mia's relentless pursuit. "This could be the proof we need."

"Good," Mia said. "We're close."

But the deeper we dug, the more the danger loomed, a

shadow stretching across my mind. Protecting Mia wasn't just a mission anymore; it was a necessity, etched into every fiber of my being.

"Careful," I said as she navigated through a particularly insidious piece of coding that reeked of a trap. "One wrong move…"

"I know." Her tone was sharp, but her eyes held trust. A trust I'd earned and one I refused to break.

Our findings painted a damning picture of Ivor's network, a web of corruption that extended farther than either of us had expected. As the final pieces clicked into place, I realized the gravity of what we were about to undertake. This was more than exposing a criminal—it was tearing down an empire.

"Look at this," Mia whispered, scrolling through a dense section of data. "This is it, Cikarius. Ivor's plans, his entire operation—it's all here."

"Compelling evidence," I said, though my mind raced with what came next—the confrontation.

"Can you trace any financial transactions?" I asked, my gaze not leaving the screen.

"Already on it." She worked the console with a fervor, her fingers coaxing secrets from the depths of the network.

"Got something," she announced triumphantly.

"Good." I felt a surge of pride. "Let's see what Ivor has been hiding."

We delved deeper, uncovering layer upon layer of deception, each revelation adding to the mosaic of corruption. It was a dangerous game we played, balancing on the edge of a knife.

A flicker of green and blue illuminated Mia's face, casting it in an eerie glow as her fingers danced over the keyboard. She hunted through the labyrinth of data with a predator's precision, and I stood sentry, watching her back. Every piece of information she found led her to something else.

"Here." Mia's voice cut through my thoughts, sharp with urgency. She pointed to a cluster of data. "Coordinates for Ivor's base on Dufair."

I leaned in closer, eyes scanning the information. No doubt it was heavily guarded. "As a Sionagog Syndicate client, Ivor will have mercenary guards until the hit is completed."

Her frown cut through the dim light. "I hate being called the hit."

"Apologies," I said. The old ways clung to me like shadows. "It will take time to unthink and unlearn all the terminology the Sionagog Syndicate put in me."

"It's okay." She turned her attention back to the computer.

But it wasn't okay. If I wanted Mia to trust me, stay with me, I had to reprogram myself. Start thinking for myself and not how they wanted me to think or act. First, I needed to confront Ivor.

"We need to be careful when we approach the base," I said.

"Why can't we just find a shuttle and go back to the station? Let the authorities take care of Ivor," she said, hopeful but naïve.

Her naïveté about the situation tugged a smile onto my lips, despite the gravity of our conversation. "Ivor will never stop coming for you. And the Sionagog Syndicate prides itself on always getting the job done." My hand found hers, an instinctive gesture. "I need Ivor to cancel the hit on you."

Doubt flickered across her face, her green eyes clouded with worry. But there was determination there too; she wasn't one to flee from a challenge. We locked eyes, the air between us charged with an understanding deeper than words. With every shared glance and touch, the bond between us grew tangled up in survival and something much more dangerous.

"Then let's make sure he gets the message," she said. "What's our next move?"

"Preparation," I said, my mind already racing with strategies and contingencies. We need supplies, information, an edge.

She eyed the computer screen where Ivor's base location blinked ominously. "He won't just let us walk in and convince him to back off. You know that, right?"

"Persuasion comes in many forms." My voice was a low hum, barely concealing the undercurrent of danger. I had ways of making men like Ivor bend to my will.

"I don't want to spend my life looking over my shoulder, Cikarius."

Her gaze locked onto mine, a silent plea echoing in those green depths. Infiltrating Ivor's lair wouldn't be easy; we'd need to consider every variable, prepare for the guards, the traps, any unforeseen dangers lurking within. Together, we plotted with purpose, driven by survival and the hope for freedom from this relentless hunt.

"I promise you won't have to."

"How are you going to get to him?" Her eyes met mine, searching for a plan.

"I'll think of something." The corners of my mouth twitched upward, a semblance of a smile. We hunched over the facility's computer, her fingers a blur across the keyboard as we mapped out our approach, considering every variable, every shadow that might hide a threat.

"Done," she said, leaning back, her ponytail brushing against the high collar of her jacket.

I shifted in my seat, turning my attention to the computer. Every computer on Dufair, Alfataken Station, and Talamhmar belonged to the same network. When the research potential of the moon was discovered, governments and scientists wanted a way to easily exchange data. But everyone used the network now, from businesses to civilians wanting to keep in touch. Its archaic interface was sluggish, the cursor blinking lazily on the screen, but it wouldn't betray us to prying digital eyes. I navigated through layers of code, finding the hidden pathway I'd left dormant within the Sionagog Syndicate's network—a backdoor known only to me.

"Access granted," the screen announced silently, and I dove into the abyss of encrypted files. Every keystroke was deliberate. My muscles tense with anticipation. I activated a failsafe program I'd created years ago—a just-in-case measure —and began downloading the Sionagog Syndicate's client list.

"What are you doing?" Mia's voice, tinged with curiosity, broke the silence.

"Insurance." The single word hung between us, weighted with unspoken promises of safety and retaliation.

"Against?"

"Uncertainty." I looked at her, and in that moment, shared more than just a look; I shared an understanding of the perilous tightrope we walked.

The information streamed into a secure digital box, its virtual locks snapping shut. I sent the box spiraling into the ether of cyberspace, where it would orbit unseen until needed.

"Ready?" Mia asked, her gaze now steady, resolve hardening like armor.

"Always," I said, feeling the pull of destiny, of fated moments yet to unfold.

As we rose from our makeshift command center, the hum of the jungle outside whispered secrets of what lay ahead. The air was charged with potential, with the promise of confrontation and the sweet tang of hope against over-whelming odds.

"Let's gather what we need," I said, scanning the dimly lit room. Mia nodded, her slender fingers deftly packing her computer and the precious flora samples into the rugged backpack. She moved with precision, every item purposefully selected for utility and necessity.

I turned my attention to the scavenging task at hand, picking through mechanical remnants, selecting parts that could be traded for passage off this forsaken moon.

We stepped out into the jungle's embrace, its bioluminescent foliage casting an otherworldly glow on our path. The air was thick, heavy with the scent of exotic flowers and damp soil, a stark contrast to the sterile corridors of Alfataken Station. I led the way, every sense heightened to detect the slightest anomaly in the symphony of wild sounds around us.

Mia followed close behind, her green eyes scanning our surroundings. "The terrain seems to be changing," she said, her voice barely above a whisper.

"Adaptability is key." I replied, noting the subtle shift in the underbrush, the way the ferns gave way to a denser thicket.

A sudden rustling to our right had us both freezing in place. I reached back, feeling Mia's steady presence just inches from mine. Her breath was calm, measured, betraying none of the adrenaline that surely coursed through her veins.

We waited, and a creature—a Dufairian shadow-slink—emerged, its iridescent scales reflecting the faint luminescence of the jungle. It eyed us warily before slithering away into the darkness, a silent testament to the dangers lurking within the luminescent wilds.

"Close one," Mia said, her voice tinged with the thrill of survival.

"Part of the journey," I responded, moving forward once more.

Our progress was slow, deliberate. We navigated through thickets of glowing vines and over roots as large as conduits, every step a dance with nature's unpredictability. Our combined knowledge of the land and my instincts as a former hit man kept us one step ahead of the myriad threats concealed by the jungle's beauty.

"Look out!" Mia's alert came just in time for me to parry a

branch, whipping towards us as if alive. My reflexes, honed from countless missions, responded instantly, and I deflected the danger away from us.

"Thank you," she said, her eyes meeting mine. In them, I saw not only gratitude but a burgeoning trust that went beyond the simple instinct to survive.

"Always," I replied, the word now taking on a new meaning—one of protection, of an unspoken vow.

The jungle seemed endless, but we pressed on, determined to reach Ivor's base before nightfall. Each challenge we faced, each obstacle we overcame, bound us closer together. With every step, I felt the weight of my past actions lifting, replaced by the burgeoning weight of responsibility for Mia's safety.

As the sun dipped below the horizon, painting the sky with streaks of fiery orange and pink, we found ourselves at the edge of a clearing. The base lay ahead, shrouded in the twilight shadows, promising both danger and answers.

"Almost there," Mia said, her hand brushing against mine —a fleeting touch, but enough to send a jolt of electricity through my body.

"Stay close," I instructed, my voice low. "It's far from over."

We crouched at the edge of the clearing, surveying Ivor's base. Its angular shapes loomed against the darkening sky, an unnatural blight amidst the organic curves of Dufair's wilderness. My eyes scanned for movement, for the telltale signs of guards or surveillance tech. Nothing stirred, but that didn't mean we were alone.

"Motion sensors, likely camouflaged," Mia said, pointing to a spot where the air shimmered ever so slightly.

"Right." I nodded. "Follow my lead."

We skirted the perimeter, every sense alert. The tang of metal and lubricant hung faintly in the air, betraying the presence of hidden machines. I caught the occasional soft hum of idling electronics, waiting to spring to life.

"There," I said, spotting a dense patch of ferns glowing softly under the moon's caress. A hidden entrance, just as the schematics had promised.

We slipped through the vegetation, the leaves brushing against us with velvet caresses. Inside, dim light bathed the corridor, sterile and cold. We moved in silence, communicating with glances and gestures honed by our shared trials.

Mia pulled out her computer, fingers dancing across the surface with practiced ease. She summoned the layout we'd stored in its memory, a holographic blueprint that hovered between us. I memorized the turns and intersections, plotting our course through the labyrinth.

"Ready?" she asked, the green of her eyes reflecting the hologram's glow.

"Always," I echoed our earlier exchange.

We navigated the corridors, blending into the shadows, our footsteps whispers on the floor, our breathing controlled. Each turn took us deeper into the heart of Ivor's lair, closer to the evidence we needed to end this hunt.

The tension wound tight within me, a spring coiled and ready to release. But alongside it, there was something else— something warmer, softer. It was the brush of Mia's hand against mine as we moved together, synchronized and attuned to each other's presence.

Then, as we rounded a corner, we froze. Ahead of us, a guard stood watch, his back turned to us. His stance spoke of complacency, unaware of the predators that now stalked him.

I looked at Mia, a silent question in my eyes. She nodded, understanding the unspoken plan. With careful precision, we advanced, ready to incapacitate, to move undetected.

But as we edged closer, the guard shifted, and the subtle clink of his armor sent a shiver down my spine. The moment teetered on the brink of disaster.

"Look out!" Mia said under her breath, pointing beyond the guard to a door flanked by two more sentries. That marked our target—the room was heavy with secrets we needed to uncover.

"Diversion," I mouthed back, and she nodded once, sharply.

I retreated, circling back to a junction where pipes climbed the walls like metal vines. My fingers found the valve we had passed earlier, and with a twist, I wrenched it open. A scream of pressurized steam erupted, a cloud billowing into the corridor, obscuring vision, muddling senses.

"Alert! Breach in sector seven!" I yelled, mimicking the grunt of the guards. It was crude, but effective.

The guards snapped to attention, radios crackling with confusion as they converged on the source of the chaos. I slipped through the dissipating mist, a phantom in their midst.

Mia seized the opportunity, darting to the now unguarded door, her movements a dance of urgency and grace. She interfaced with the panel, fingers flying over the controls, her concentration absolute.

"Almost there," she said, the door's lock cycling with an audible click.

We slipped inside the room beyond a vault of data waiting to be plundered. And as we began our work, I couldn't help but marvel at the woman beside me—her intellect as formidable as any weapon I'd ever wielded.

"Got it," she whispered triumphantly, her screen alive with incriminating evidence.

"Let's not celebrate yet," I said, glancing at the door, aware that each passing second increased our risk of discovery.

"Right," she said, a flicker of determination steeling her features. "Then let's make this quick."

The glow of the console painted her in strokes of light and

shadow, casting her in an otherworldly aura. Her focus was a tangible force, and I stood sentinel, watching over her as she worked to extract the data that could seal Ivor's fate—and perhaps ensure our survival.

As she downloaded the last file, a sound from the hallway caught my attention. Footsteps—returning. A surge of adrenaline hit me, and I moved without thought, positioning myself between Mia and the impending threat.

"Time to go," I said, the primal need to protect her eclipsing all else.

"Done," she said, unplugging her device with haste.

We exited just as the first guard rounded the corner, his shout of alarm slicing through the air. But we were already ghosts, slipping away into the maze of corridors, the data our lifeline, the thrill of escape lending wings to our feet.

CHAPTER 10
CIKARIUS

"Data, Mia. Do you have all of it?"

We didn't have much time before the guards tracked us down. We needed to get out of there.

"Yes, I think so."

"Find a hiding spot," I said. "I'll track down Ivor."

Mia's response was visceral—a look that seared into me, a mixture of revulsion and defiance. I had been an assassin. To her, I was still stained with the blood of countless contracts.

Her lips thinned, the corners set in determination. "I'm safer with you," she said, her voice low but fierce.

"Understood." There was no room for argument when survival was at stake. We continued down the corridor lit by the flickering neon lights.

The hum of machinery thrummed through the walls, mingling with the distant echoes of voices lost in the labyrinthine bowels of the base. It was a stark contrast to the wild chorus of Dufair's jungle, where this had all begun. The metallic tang of the recycled air bit at the back of my throat.

As we edged closer to the main hub, the tension strung tight like the strings of a bow ready to snap. I reached for

Mia's hand, feeling the softness of her skin against the callouses of my own—a silent promise of protection.

"Stay alert," I whispered, every sense sharpened to the possibility of danger lurking around each corner.

"Always am," she said, her grip firm, betraying none of the fear that must have been coursing through her.

We moved as one entity, a symbiosis born of necessity, yet underpinned by something deeper, something unspoken that crackled between us like a static charge. Every step measured, every breath synchronized as we closed in on our quarry.

But as we approached the heart of the facility, I knew the true test was upon us. With Ivor close, escape was a dream fraying at the edges, about to be torn apart by the harsh claws of reality.

"Ready?" I asked, pausing before the entrance to the main hub, my hand hovering over the blaster at my side.

"Let's end this," Mia said, steel in her tone, her expression resolute.

I pulled a spider-cam from the pouch at my belt, its legs twitched as I set it down. With a swift command, the device skittered forward, disappearing beneath the closed door of Ivor's command center. The camera feed flickered to life on my wrist display, the grainy images painting a grim tableau.

Ivor Atreus stood, arrogance personified in his tailored suit, posture relaxed yet commanding. Beside him, a shadow detached from the wall—Griff Halden, muscles coiled, eyes sharp as flint. My heart sank like a stone in deep water; Griff was loyalty and lethality, wrapped in one imposing package.

"Damn," I cursed under my breath, watching the mercenary's every move through the camera's eye.

"What is it?" Mia's voice was a whisper, her face a mask of concern in the dim corridor light.

"Griff," I said, the name tasting like bile. "The best mercenary in the sector, and he's glued to Ivor's side."

Her eyes widened, understanding the weight of the situation as she peered over my shoulder at the display.

"Can we get past him?"

"Griff's not someone you simply 'get past'," I replied, feeling the weight of my respect for the man clash with the imperative need to protect Mia. "But I'll do what I must."

"Then what's the plan?" She tucked a loose strand of hair behind her ear, a small act of defiance against the chaos that awaited us.

"Stay out of sight, stay alive." I locked eyes with her, trying to convey all the things I couldn't say out loud. "If things go bad, I want you hidden. Promise me that."

Her nod was firm, but her lips pressed into a thin line. I knew she hated the idea of staying back, but this wasn't the time for arguments.

"Promise," she whispered.

"Good." I took a deep breath, the recycled air of the facility filling my lungs, smelling faintly of metal and fear. "Let's go."

We crept closer, our shadows merging with the darkness as we approached the door. My hand hovered above the panel, ready to key in the sequence that would bring us face-to-face with destiny. A shiver ran down my spine, anticipation and dread mingling like bitter cocktails in my veins.

"Stay close," I said, and with a last glance at Mia, whose determination mirrored my own, I pressed the button.

The door slid open with a quiet hiss.

The room was a maelstrom of activity, the hum of machinery and staccato beeps of consoles creating a discordant symphony. But every sound faded to silence as we burst in. Me—a towering figure clad in black—and Mia, following close behind before ducking beneath a desk.

"She's supposed to be dead." Ivor's voice cut through the tension, his finger pointing directly at Mia's chosen hiding spot. His silhouette loomed like a specter over the array of monitors that bathed him in an eerie glow.

"Keep quiet," I mouthed to Mia, my eyes never leaving Ivor. She nodded, her green eyes wide but resolute.

Griff stepped forward, blocking Ivor's view, his imposing form a testament to battles fought and survived. "What brings you here, Cikarius? You rarely meet with the client in person."

"Step out of the way." My voice was calm, measured, but the edge was there, sharp enough to slice through the charged atmosphere. "I don't want to kill you, but I will if I have to." The memory of past camaraderie with Griff flashed, unwelcome. Now was not the time for sentimentality.

"Can't do that," he said, the hint of regret in his tone almost imperceptible.

"Then it'll be your last mistake." I narrowed my eyes at Ivor. "You're going to withdraw the contract on Mia."

Ivor's laugh was bitter and hollow. "Not likely."

The air between us crackled, charged with the inevitability of conflict. I could feel Mia's gaze on us, her presence both a comfort and a reminder of what was at stake.

"Last chance, Ivor." My hand hovered near the weapon concealed within my coat, ready to draw in one fluid motion.

"Make me," Ivor sneered, confident in his stronghold.

"Very well," I said, and in the next heartbeat, the room erupted into chaos.

I pulled the evidence from my coat, a thin data-slate that glowed faintly against the dim lighting of Ivor's command center. With a flick of my wrist, the images and documents of his treachery splashed across the wall: transactions, communications, all pointing to one undeniable fact—Ivor Atreus was guilty.

"Corporate espionage, Ivor? And the hit on Mia—" Griff scanned the evidence, disbelief etching lines into his weathered face. "You told me the contract was on a gang leader supplying weapons to kids."

"Griff," Ivor began, his voice dipped in honeyed tones of reassurance, "you know how these things can be misconstrued. Documents can be forged; images altered."

"Step out of the way," I repeated, ignoring Ivor's attempts at deceit. The air felt heavy, thick with the scent of ozone and tension.

"Does she look like a gang leader to you?" I asked Griff, motioning toward the desk. "Mia, stand up."

She rose slowly, her silhouette framed by the pulsating screens behind her. Her green eyes locked onto Griff's, an unspoken plea within them.

"I'm a botanist working for Ivor's competition," she said, her voice steady despite the situation.

"Enough." Ivor's attempt at maintaining an air of control was slipping as he glanced nervously between us. "This is preposterous. Cikarius has always been a loose cannon. Are we really going to believe the word of a genetically engineered weapon who's abandoned his own kind?"

"Is that so?" My response was cool, unflinching. I stepped closer, the data-slate in hand, presenting cold, hard facts that left no room for doubt. "The timestamps don't lie, Ivor. Your transactions coincide perfectly with cyber attacks on her employer's computers. Mia's only crime was being too good at her job."

Griff shifted, the weight of the truth settling onto his shoulders. He glanced from Ivor to Mia, then back to me. The standoff teetered on the brink—the next move would tip the scales.

"Think about it, Griff. You've been played." The words hung in the air, a final testament to Ivor's deceit.

The moonlight filtered through the windows, casting long shadows on the floor, mirroring the darkness that had settled over us. In the corner of the room, the soft hum of machinery underscored the silence that followed.

"Let's end this," I said, a silent prayer that Griff would make the right choice.

The tension was a live wire, ready to ignite. Every sense was heightened—the metallic taste of anticipation on my tongue, the sound of distant footsteps echoing like a countdown, the smell of fear mingling with determination.

"Griff?" Ivor's voice was barely a whisper, laced with the poison of betrayal.

We waited, breaths held, as the moment stretched into infinity.

Griff's eyes, hard as the steel of his blade, met mine. The mercenary who had faced down death without flinching now stood at a crossroads, his allegiance tested. His jaw clenched; the decision written in the tightening of his fists.

"Your move, Griff," Ivor said, voice smooth as silk and just as suffocating.

The mercenary's gaze flickered to Mia, her presence a silent accusation, a beacon of truth amidst the murk of lies. He took a step back, not in surrender but in defiance, aligning himself beside me without uttering a word.

"Damn you," Ivor spat, the façade crumbling. He tapped his wrist device with a fury that betrayed his composure.

I braced myself, every muscle tensed for what was to come. The door burst open behind Ivor, and a squadron of mercenaries poured into the room like a flood of dark intent.

"Circle up!" I said, pulling Mia close. My hand found the grip of my weapon with practiced ease.

Griff moved like a shadow, fluid and deadly, positioning himself back-to-back with me. The air crackled with the electricity of impending combat, the weight of destiny pressing down upon us.

"Take them!" Ivor commanded, his voice slicing through the tension.

Silent understanding passed between Griff and me. We were warriors forged in different fires, now tempered by a common cause. The mercenaries advanced, a closing ring of malice.

"Stay behind me," I whispered to Mia, hoping she could feel the promise in my words. Her soft exhale brushed against my neck, a whisper of trust amidst the chaos.

The first assailant lunged, a blur of motion aimed at my heart. I sidestepped, turning his momentum against him, my hand striking with lethal precision. He crumpled to the ground, a silent testament to my resolve.

"Watch out!" Griff's warning came just in time, his arm knocking aside an attack meant for my side.

We moved as one, a dance of destruction under the cold glow of florescent lights. Sweat beaded on my brow. The scent of metal and fear filled the air, and the sounds of combat—the clash of weapons, the thud of bodies—became a symphony of survival.

A surge of adrenaline coursed through me as I caught the glint of a blade swinging towards my face. With a swift pivot, I caught the wrist of the mercenary, turning the momentum to send him sprawling. His weapon clattered across the floor, slipping into the darkness.

"Go, Mia! Now!" My voice was a command, an anchor in the storm of violence swirling around us. I needed her safe, needed her brilliance shielded from the brutality that was my world.

Out of the corner of my eye, through a haze of exertion, I saw her silhouette darting toward the console. Her fingertips darted from key to key, a dance of urgency and intelligence. The screen flickered, data streaming through the ether to her boss, her salvation—and mine—within reach.

Another attacker charged, his snarl lost in the cacophony. I met him head-on, my fist connecting with a satisfying crunch against his jaw. He staggered, surprise etching his features before he collapsed.

"Good work," Griff said beside me, taking down another assailant with calculated ferocity. Despite the chaos, a part of me appreciated the irony—Griff, once a potential enemy, was now an ally by choice.

The room echoed with the clash of combat, every strike a note in our desperate symphony. I fought not just for survival but for a future that, until recently, I hadn't dared to envision —one where Mia was more than just a mission, more than just a target. She was the unexpected variable that had recalculated my entire existence.

"Data's sent!" Mia's triumphant cry cut through the fray, a beacon of hope.

"Stay down!" I called out, taking down another mercenary. My body moved on instinct, each movement honed by years of training, each breath a testament to my newfound purpose.

And then it was over. The last of Ivor's mercenaries lay defeated at my feet, their bodies a testament to the deadly skills that had once defined me. But now, standing amid the wreckage of battle, I felt reborn—a protector forged from the ashes of an assassin.

My gaze found Mia, her eyes wide with a mix of fear and admiration. In that moment, as our eyes locked, something unspoken passed between us. A silent vow that no matter what came next, her life was mine to defend.

"Time to make this right," I growled, advancing on Ivor, who cowered against the wall, his bravado evaporated.

"What are you going to do?" Ivor asked.

"Rescind it," I demanded, my voice a low growl.

Ivor hesitated, a flicker of uncertainty crossing his sharp features. Trying to assess my next move. In all the years I'd been a hit man, a contract had only been rescinded twice.

With a movement swift as the predatory creatures of this moon, I seized his arm, pressing the cold muzzle of my plasma pistol against his temple. He swallowed, and his Adam's apple bobbed under the coercion of undeniable defeat.

"Fine," Ivor spat out, and his fingers slogged over his wrist device with a reluctance that tasted like venom on my genetically enhanced tongue. My device buzzed against my skin, the contract cancellation flashing up with sterile finality. A sigh escaped me, relief mingling with the understanding that there would be no turning back.

"Thank you," I said, meaning it.

Despite Ivor's fear, the arms dealer glared at me.

"Goodbye, Ivor." My voice was devoid of emotion, a perfect reflection of the void where my humanity should have been. Yet, as I pulled the trigger, extinguishing the life of the man who marked Mia for death, I felt a surge of something fierce and protective, an emotion that transcended my genetically engineered origins.

Ivor crumpled to the ground, the sound of his body hitting the hard floor drowned by the shocked gasps from Mia and Griff. The deed was done. I turned back to Mia, my heart beating to the rhythm of her name. She looked at me, her expression a complex weave of terror, gratitude, and something deeper, more intimate.

Griff frowned, surveying the room, his loyalty to the Sionagog Syndicate now a distant memory compared to the justice unfolding before him. "He cancelled the contract."

"Yes." My voice was steady, the decision made long before Ivor's death. "And the second I let him go, he'd issue another one." There was no place for mercy on this battlefield, not when Mia's life hung in the balance.

A rustle of movement, and Mia was there, running into my arms. Her warmth against my body was a stark contrast to the cold resolve that still pulsed through my veins. She clung to me, her presence a soothing balm to the adrenaline that had yet to ebb from my system.

"Thank you," she said against my chest, her words carrying the weight of our shared ordeal.

"We're not out of the woods yet," I said, aware of the many dangers still lurking in the shadows of Dufair. "But you're safe—for now."

Her breath hitched, a silent echo of my own racing heart. Pulling back slightly, Mia searched my eyes, and I saw the reflection of my turmoil mirrored in hers. Our lips met in an intimate and passionate kiss, the taste of her mingling with the metallic tang of battle still fresh on my tongue. The scent of her hair, a faint reminder of the luminescent flora she adored, cut through the acrid smoke that lingered in the air.

The kiss deepened, and the world around us faded into obscurity. There was only Mia, with her soft curves pressed against the hard lines of my body. Her hands roamed over the contours of my back, tracing the muscles honed by years of combat, now tensed with a different kind of anticipation.

"Look at what we've done," she said, pulling away just enough to gesture at the chaos surrounding us. The fallen mercenaries, the blinking lights on the consoles, the distant hum of machinery.

"We did what we had to," I said, my voice rough with emotion. "But it's not over yet."

Her eyes, green and alive with a fire that matched the bioluminescent canopy outside, held mine. In them, I saw more than gratitude—I saw a shared victory, a bond forged in the crucible of danger that neither of us could deny.

"Let's get out of here," I said, already scanning for the quickest escape route. "We have evidence to deliver, and a galaxy to convince."

Mia nodded, resolve steeling her delicate features. "Together."

"Always," I promised, sealing our pact with another searing kiss that spoke of battles yet to come and nights spent in each other's arms. "We'll continue this once we're safe on the station."

CHAPTER 11
MIA

Stepping off the spacecraft, my heart raced as I took in the bustling atmosphere of Alfataken Station's arrival area. Cikarius stood tall beside me, his violet skin and glowing yellow eyes drawing curious glances from passersby. I clutched my backpack containing the precious samples from Dufair's luminescent flora and the computer that held incriminating evidence against Ivor. The bag never left my side.

"Security clearance is going to be tough," I said, my voice wavering. Cikarius squeezed my hand reassuringly, his firm grip a reminder of the countless times he had protected me during our perilous journey.

"Trust me, Mia. We'll get through this." His deep voice soothed my nerves, a hint of warmth beneath the usual frosty tone.

We made our way to the customs clearance area, our steps synced, determined. The line moved quickly, and it was our turn to face the station official. He looked us over, his eyes lingering on Cikarius's imposing figure before scanning our identification and travel documents.

"Your purpose on Dufair?" he asked, his voice monotone.

"Work." My voice was steady, despite the pounding in my chest. "I'm a botanist."

Cikarius's grip tightened. "Her bodyguard." His gaze locked with the official's.

The man's gaze slid to Cikarius, lingering on his violet skin and inhuman eyes. After a long moment, he handed our documents back with a curt nod.

"Welcome home."

Relief flooded me as we strode into the station, the familiar scents of metal and ozone filling my senses. Cikarius pulled me close against his side, his warmth seeping into me and easing the tension in my muscles.

"See? I told you we'd make it through," he said as we walked further into the station, his eyes sweeping the area for potential threats.

"Thank you, Cikarius. I couldn't have done this without you." I smiled up at him, my heart swelling with gratitude and something deeper—a connection that had grown between us despite the danger that surrounded our every step.

"Anything for you, Mia." His eyes softened, the ever-present coldness momentarily lifted by the warmth of our shared bond. And as we ventured deeper into Alfataken Station, a shred of hope bloomed in this new, uncertain world we were about to face together.

Suddenly, my communication device vibrated with an incoming message. I glanced at the screen and saw that it was from Caelum, my boss. With a mix of curiosity and apprehension, I opened the message.

> Take all the time you need. Your safety and well-being are our top priority. We'll handle things here while you're away.

A wave of relief washed over me as I finished reading Caelum's supportive words. The weight on my shoulders lifted, knowing that my boss understood my situation and was giving me the time and space I needed.

I fired off a quick response.

> Thanks. We have so much to talk about when I return.

"Good news?" Cikarius asked, his voice filled with genuine concern.

"Very," I said, showing him the message. He scanned it quickly and nodded in approval.

"Seems like we've got some time to figure things out," he said, the tension in his muscles easing slightly.

I glanced up at him, losing myself in the glow of his yellow eyes. "You promised we'd continue what we started in Ivor's base. But this isn't exactly private."

A faint smirk curled his mouth. "Your quarters are nearby. And I fully intend to make good on that promise, my love."

He paused for a moment, lost in thought, before making a decision. "Since I'm done with the Sionagog Syndicate," he said, "maybe I could become a mercenary instead, work alongside Griff."

The idea of Cikarius abandoning his life as a hit man and starting anew sent a thrill down my spine. Together, we could face whatever challenges lay ahead, forging our own path through this dangerous world.

As we walked hand in hand towards my - our - quarters on Alfataken Station, anticipation and a sense of new beginnings pulsed through me. Our eyes met, bound by love, trust, and the promise of a future we would create together.

Stepping into our quarters, a sense of intimacy and privacy immediately enveloped us. The soft lighting cast warm shadows on the walls, and the faint hum of the station's machinery seemed to fade away, leaving only our breaths and heartbeats as company.

Cikarius pulled me into his arms, one hand cradling the back of my head as he gazed down at me. "You're safe now. No one will hurt you again, not as long as I live."

His vow resonated through me, chasing away the last shadows of fear and doubt. Here in the circle of his embrace, I felt secure, knowing that he would always protect me.

"I can never thank you enough for saving me," I whispered, taking Cikarius's hand and guiding him towards the bed. "I'm yours. Forever."

His eyes filled with desire as he looked at me—my violet phantom, my protector, my love. Without another word, he shed his clothes, revealing the muscular body that had shielded me from harm time and time again. My gaze was drawn to his already hard cock, my hands aching to touch him, to feel the heat and power of his body beneath my fingertips.

"Let me show you my gratitude," I said, as we moved closer until there was no space left between us.

His lips claimed mine in a searing kiss, and I moaned softly as his tongue swept into my mouth. Every nerve in my body came alive under his touch, my core aching with need. I tangled my fingers in his hair, kissing him back fiercely.

When we finally broke apart, panting, I gazed up at him through half-lidded eyes. "I want you, Cikarius. Now."

A low growl rumbled in his chest. "I thought you'd never ask."

Cikarius undressed me, his hands delicately tracing patterns on my skin as he removed each article of clothing. I shivered with delight at every touch, feeling alive, desired, and protected all at once. When I stood naked before him, I knew that there was nothing more I wanted than to share this intimate connection with him—body and soul.

He lifted me and carried me to the bed, laying me out before him like an offering. I trembled in anticipation, drinking in the sight of his lean, muscular body and the rigid length of his cock.

Cikarius prowled toward me, desire darkening his gaze. "You're mine to claim now."

"Yes," I said, opening myself to him in invitation.

Our lips met in a deep, passionate kiss, Cikarius's tongue sweeping into my mouth, exploring its depths and entwining with mine in an electrifying dance. Sensations rippled through my entire body, every nerve singing with pleasure as he continued to lavish attention upon me.

He moved his kisses lower, his lips leaving a trail of fire down my neck, across my collarbone, and towards my breasts. As he reached them, he attended to each one with equal ardor, sucking greedily at my nipples while his hands gently caressed their curves. My stomach fluttered with desire, my heart hammering wildly in my chest as if trying to match the intensity of our shared passion.

Cikarius continued his exploration, his lips and tongue tracing a path down my body. He settled between my thighs, his warm breath teasing against my sensitive skin. His tongue darted out to lick my clit, sending a jolt of pleasure through me that made me arch off the bed and moan loudly.

"Please, Cikarius, fuck me," I begged, the words spilling out in a breathless whisper.

He chuckled softly, his eyes filled with burning desire as he looked up at me. "That is a command I will gladly obey," he said. "But why rush when we can take our time?"

Cikarius moved back up my body, his firm, muscled form pressing against mine. His cock teased at my entrance, causing me to shiver in anticipation. As his lips met mine once more, his tongue stroking and caressing my own, he simultaneously teased me with the promise of his cock at the entrance to my core.

Cikarius stretched out beside me, one hand skimming up my side to cup my breast. I arched into his touch with a soft moan, craving more of his skillful caresses. Our gazes locked, glowing yellow to vibrant green, as unspoken words of love and desire passed between us.

"Now you're just torturing me."

"But what delicious torture it is," Cikarius said. The grin on his face shot a jolt of arousal to my core.

Cikarius cupped my face in his hands, gazing at me with a tender reverence that made my heart ache with joy. No words were needed in this moment - our connection went far deeper than mere speech. I leaned up to brush my lips against his, a feather-light caress that sent sparks of pleasure dancing across my skin. He let out a soft groan, wrapping his arms around me and pulling me flush against him.

He kissed me, his tongue caressing mine, each stroke fueled by passion and longing. I reveled in the feel of his body against mine, hard muscle and sinew molding to my softer curves. His arousal pressed against my thigh, hot and insistent, eliciting a surge of desire that left me trembling. I wanted nothing more than to give myself over to him completely, to unite our bodies as profoundly as our souls.

Cikarius trailed kisses along my jaw and down the curve of my neck, nipping and sucking at my pulse point. I arched into him with a breathy sigh, hands sliding across the planes of his back. He grasped my hips and ground against me, dragging a strangled moan from my throat. The exquisite friction set every nerve in my body alight, coiling pleasure within my core. I was already slick and aching for him, desperate to be filled in the way only he could satisfy.

"Please," I said, clinging to him as another wave of arousal crashed over me. Cikarius lifted his head, eyes glowing with a predatory hunger. A smirk curled his lips that sent a thrill of danger and excitement through me. In this moment, I was his to devour - and devour me he would.

"How can I deny such a heartfelt plea?" he asked, voice rough with lust. And then he was kissing me again, and all thought fled as I gave myself over to sweet oblivion in his arms.

He shifted between my thighs, the broad head of his cock nudging at my entrance. I arched into him with a wordless plea, wrapping my legs around his waist to draw him closer. Cikarius slid into me in one smooth thrust, stretching and filling me so perfectly I saw stars. We moaned in unison, a harmony of pleasure that sang through my veins.

For a moment we remained still, savoring the feeling of being joined so intimately. Cikarius gazed down at me with a tenderness that made my heart ache, brushing a stray lock of hair from my face. I traced the angular lines of his jaw and the curve of his lips, overcome by a surge of love and desire so powerful it stole my breath. No matter how many times we came together, the depth of my feelings for him never ceased to humble and astonish me.

He began to move then, rolling his hips in a slow rhythm that quickly unraveled my restraint. I met each thrust eagerly, desire building within me like the swell of an ocean tide. Cikarius gripped my hips, guiding me to a tempo that had us both gasping. The familiar pressure coiled low in my belly, sending ripples of ecstasy throughout my body.

"Mia," he groaned, burying his face against my neck. His thrusts grew harder, deeper, spurred on by the sounds of my pleasure. I clung to him, nails scoring down his back as the coil within me threatened to burst. Cikarius shuddered, hips stuttering as he found his release - and with a cry, the coil unapped, sending me tumbling into bliss.

The orgasm crashed over me, so intense it took my breath away. Pulse after pulse echoed across my body, leaving my skin super sensitive to the touch.

We lay entwined for a long moment, our harsh breathing the only sound in the room. I traced idle patterns across Cikarius's skin, savoring the warmth of his body against mine. His arms tightened around me in response, a silent affirmation of the bond we now shared.

"You are mine, as I am yours," he said, echoing words spoken in the heart of the jungle that seemed a lifetime ago. I tilted my head up, meeting his gaze with a smile. "I love you, Mia."

My heart leaped at his admission. "I love you, too."

"Always."

Cikarius claimed my lips in a searing kiss, full of promise and passion. I gave myself over to it without reservation, certain in the knowledge that we would face any challenge the future held - together.

When at last we parted, I nestled against his chest again, listening to the strong and steady beat of his heart. A sense of peace settled over me as I drifted off to sleep in the shelter of his embrace, our destinies now and forever entwined on this space station we called home.

VILLAINS DO IT BETTER

Embark on an unforgettable adventure with these incredible authors as they transport you to worlds and galaxies beyond imagination—where good doesn't always wear white and bad has never been so tempting.

Aliens. Shifters. Vampires. Demons. Explore the dark and the dangerous with creatures who lurk in shadows and prove that villains always bring the heat.

If *Rescued by the Alien Hit Man* captured your heart, don't miss the other thrilling stories in this morally gray collection.

www.villainsdoitbetter.com

JOIN MARS' ALIEN TEMPTATIONS

Join my mailing list, Mars' Alien Temptations (https://terrynmars.com/newsletter) for sneak peeks, behind-the-scenes content, and more. It's where I chat about how the books are coming along, announce new releases, do cover reveals. I hope to see you over there!

Terryn

ALSO BY TERRYN MARS

Princes of Dagelax Series

Alien Affair

Alien Liaison

ABOUT THE AUTHOR

Terryn Mars writes sizzling science fiction romance that always has a happily ever after. From a young age astronomy fascinated her. She often wondered what might be out there among the billions of stars. Now she gets to let her imagination soar writing tales of human women finding love with alien heroes.

facebook.com/TerrynMars

instagram.com/terrynmars

bsky.app/profile/terrynmars.bsky.social

bookbub.com/authors/terryn-mars